UNDER PRESSURE

The first Hawks novel

TONY BRADMAN

CORGI BOOKS

UNDER PRESSURE
A CORGI BOOK : 0 552 547603

First publication in Great Britain

PRINTING HISTORY
Corgi edition published 2002

1 3 5 7 9 10 8 6 4 2

Set in 12/15.5pt Palatino by
Phoenix Typesetting, Ilkley, West Yorkshire.

Corgi Books are published by Random House Children's Books,
61–63 Uxbridge Road, London W5 5SA,
a division of The Random House Group Ltd,
in Australia by Random House Australia (Pty) Ltd,
20 Alfred Street, Milsons Point, Sydney, NSW 2061, Australia,
in New Zealand by Random House New Zealand Ltd,
18 Poland Road, Glenfield, Auckland 10, New Zealand
and in South Africa by Random House (Pty) Ltd,
Endulini, 5a Jubilee Road, Parktown 2193, South Africa.

Printed and bound in Great Britain by
Bookmarque Ltd, Croydon, Surrey.

FOR TOM AND HIS TEAM-MATES,
FROM THEIR MOST DEDICATED SUPPORTER

Like one, that on a lonesome road
Doth walk in fear and dread,
And having once turned round walks on,
And turns no more his head;
Because he knows a frightful fiend
Doth close behind him tread.

Samuel Taylor Coleridge

PROLOGUE

A silver Volvo estate comes through the open gates of Hawks' Nest, the City FC training ground, and stops in the car park. A tall, sandy-haired man gets out, bleeps the doors locked, waves to a groundsman puttering across the far pitch on a motor mower in the September sunshine. The tall man goes into a long, low building, walks past empty, echoing changing rooms, a physio suite, a gym, enters a small office. He hangs his jacket behind the door, drops his keys onto a battered desk, switches on an electric kettle. He picks up a mug bearing the words THE GAFFER, *dumps a teabag and three sugars in it, fills it with boiling water, adds milk. Then he sits down, opens a blue folder on the desk, pulls out a sheaf of forms. He glances at the small photos of boys clipped to the top of each one, finally reaching a note from Roy Newton saying the acceptance and rejection letters are being sent that day. The man looks up at a row of youth squad photos on the wall. A few of those fresh young faces made it to the big time, he thinks. Most didn't. But there are some good prospects in this new intake . . . So what did the future hold for them? We'll see, thinks Jimmy Shepherd, City FC's Youth Coach, sipping his hot, sweet tea. We'll see . . .*

ONE

Craig was sitting at the kitchen table eating his Honey Nut Flakes when the letter came. The radio was on, tuned to a pop station as usual, but he still heard the morning post thump heavily on the doormat. Craig paused, his spoon halfway to his mouth. His stomach had suddenly started doing somersaults, but the rest of him seemed to have frozen solid. He couldn't even bring himself to turn round and look at what was lying in the hall.

Craig's mum was sitting opposite him, dressed for work in a crisp white top and a dark skirt. She looked at him, raising her eyebrows till they almost touched the fringe of her neatly cut, short blond hair. She stood up, walked out of the kitchen, returned holding half a dozen white and brown envelopes.

She sat down at the table and started sorting through them. 'Bill . . . bank statement . . . bill . . . junk mail . . . bill,' she said, Craig's eyes following the envelopes as she tossed most of them unopened onto the table, until one remained in her hand. 'And last, but definitely not least,' she went on, smiling, 'a letter addressed to – a certain Master Craig Hurst . . .'

Mum held the slim white envelope towards him. Craig placed his spoon in his bowl and gingerly took the letter from her. He stared at his name and address on the front for a moment, then slowly turned the envelope over. The familiar black-and-red City crest was embossed on the back.

'Come on, Craig,' said Mum. 'I have to be at work some time today.'

Craig felt sick, but he carefully opened the envelope, eased out the sheet of paper it contained, unfolded it. He couldn't quite focus on it at first, but gradually the words stopped dancing, and he read through them. Twice.

'Well?' said Mum, sounding worried. She leaned forward. 'What does it say? For heaven's sake, Craig, I don't think I can stand the tension.'

'I'm in,' said Craig softly, and looked at her. Then the full force of what he'd just read hit him, and he leapt to his feet, his chair clattering backwards. *'I'm in, I'm in, I'm in!'* he chanted, capering wildly round the kitchen.

'Show me, then!' said Mum, chasing him. She grabbed the letter and scanned it. ' "Dear Craig . . . after your recent trial . . . delighted to offer you a place in the City youth squad . . . introductory meeting for the new season's intake and parents next Wednesday evening . . . yours sincerely, Roy Newton, Education and Welfare Executive." Oh, Craig,' she added, hugging him, dancing up and down too. 'I'm so pleased for you. It's *brilliant*.'

'Thanks, Mum,' he said when she released him. He took the letter from her, pulled his chair up, and sat down. Then he shovelled soggy Honey Nut Flakes into his mouth while he read those wonderful words once more, and Mum chattered about looking forward to telling everyone at the office.

Craig could hardly believe it. The whole thing seemed like a fantasy. He'd always loved football, and he'd been a fan of City – otherwise known as the Hawks – for as long as he could remember. Then a City scout had come to watch his school under-13s playing their first game of the season, Craig had scored a hat trick, the scout had spoken to Mr Taylor, his coach . . . And *bingo*! Craig had a place on a professional club's youth scheme. Not just any old club, either – this was *City's* youth squad, and City, of course, were in the Premiership, had been for the last three seasons. So it wasn't really anything like a fantasy, Craig decided. It was a dream come true.

Although there was a problem, Craig thought, suddenly feeling a little deflated, a worry that had been bugging him since the trial at the City training ground. And the time had arrived for him to do something about it. But he knew raising the subject with Mum wasn't going to be easy.

Craig gulped down a final mouthful of Honey Nut Flakes, then glanced round at his mum. She had finished her muesli, and now she was humming happily to herself as she studied the City FC calendar that hung on the wall beside the fridge. Mum was very organized, and wrote everything on it – school-term dates, parents' evenings, doctor's appointments, birthdays. 'There's nothing else happening next Wednesday, thank goodness,' she said, smiling. 'I'll leave work early so I'll have time to make us a proper meal before we go. But that's OK, I don't think I'm going to be busy next week . . .'

'Mum, can we ask Dad to come with us?' Craig said quickly.

Mum stopped humming and turned to face him, her smile gone. 'And why on earth would we want to do that?' she asked.

Craig didn't reply immediately, even though he knew exactly why he wanted his dad to be at the introductory meeting. There had been a few mums at the trial, but Craig had soon realized he was the only boy who'd been brought by a mum on her own. Every other lad playing that day had been supported by a dad shouting advice from the touchline. But not Craig.

Mum had often come alone to watch him play for his primary school team, and it hadn't seemed to matter then. Probably because the coach had been a lady teacher, and the team had been mixed, with girls playing as well as boys, and loads of mums coming to watch. But it mattered now, thought Craig. The City youth squad was much more, well . . . male, and Craig wasn't sure he could get through it without his dad's support. Although he couldn't explain that to his mum. He didn't think she would understand.

'I'd just, er . . . like him to be there, I suppose,' Craig mumbled at last. 'I mean, it's for the new intake and parents,' he added, pointing at the relevant line in the letter, and emphasizing the 's' at the end of the word.

Mum narrowed her eyes, looked hard at him for a long moment. Craig began to feel uncomfortable. It was almost as if she could see right through his skull and into his brain. So maybe she knew what he was thinking after all, he thought. Mum sighed, came over to the table, started briskly clearing away the breakfast dishes. Craig jumped up to help.

'I can't say the idea fills me with joy,' she muttered as she put their dirty mugs and bowls into the dishwasher and slammed the door shut. 'You know how . . . difficult things were between your father and me after the divorce. It's been over four years now, and we still haven't sorted everything out. And he's not particularly good at keeping in touch with you, is he?'

'No, Mum,' said Craig quietly, slipping their mats in the drawer. She didn't need to tell him again how tough things had been, or that his dad had put her off men so much she said she never wanted another boyfriend or husband. He knew all that. What had happened had been hard for Craig to deal with, too. He crossed his fingers behind his back, waited for her to continue.

'But I suppose if you feel you need your dad there . . .' she said at last, 'I shouldn't argue. You can call him after dinner tonight.' Craig grinned, but Mum gave him one of her warning looks.

'Don't get too excited, though. You know what he's like – he probably won't be able to make it for some reason or other. Come on, we'd better get cracking or you'll be late for school.'

They always went by car, and twenty minutes later Mum was indicating, then easing their Saxo free of the rush-hour traffic. She stopped at the corner of the street where she usually dropped Craig off. The sun was shining in a cloudless blue sky, and the pavement was crowded with kids. Craig opened his door and got out, making sure his mum didn't get a chance to kiss him. 'Bye, Mum,' he said, turning to walk away towards school.

'Hang on, Craig,' she said, leaning across the passenger seat, looking at him through the open window. Craig waited. 'You know, I really am proud of you, love,' she went on, her green eyes shining. 'Very proud.'

'Leave it out, Mum,' Craig mumbled crossly. Some boys from the year above were walking by and staring. He only hoped they hadn't heard her call him something as seriously uncool as *love*. 'I'll see you tonight.'

He strode off down the street, embarrassed, but smiling a little, too. The letter in his jacket pocket had made him feel pretty proud of himself as well. He couldn't wait to get home, phone

Dad and tell him about it . . . Craig was sure his dad would be very impressed, whatever Mum might think.

Then Craig saw a small stone on the pavement just in front of him, and couldn't resist the temptation. He dribbled it through the gates, took it round the boys from the year above, thwacked it into a bush by the bike sheds. 'He shoots, he scores!' he said to himself, and grinned happily.

'Loser,' one of the older boys hissed at him, and the others laughed and jeered, jostling him roughly as they went past. A couple of them gobbed in his direction too, just missing his shoes. Craig took no notice. They were nothing but a bunch of losers themselves, he thought, confidence surging through him.

With Dad backing him up, he thought, what could possibly go wrong?

TWO

Darren shut the front door and dumped his bag in the hall. The house was quiet, but then it often was when he got back from school, with Mum and Dad still at work, and his younger sisters at Gran and Grandad's place. Gran only worked part time, so most days she collected Ashleigh and Gemma at their junior school, gave them some tea, brought them home at six o'clock.

Not that Darren really minded being on his own. In fact, he liked the grown-up feeling it gave him, the sense that he was the one in charge of the Kimble household for once, that he could make the decisions. Then his stomach rumbled, and he headed for the kitchen to make his first major decision of the evening. What should he have for his after-school snack?

Darren opened the fridge – and his shoulders sagged. It was practically empty, apart from a tired old lettuce, a carton of half-fat milk and a tub of Flora. He'd forgotten it was Thursday. Mum and Dad did the weekly shop on Fridays, and recently they'd been cutting back to save money. So there were no treats to eat after school, and come Thursday there wasn't much left at all.

At least there was half a loaf in the bread bin. Darren dropped a couple of slices into the toaster, got the Marmite out of the cupboard, poured some milk into his favourite Arsenal mug. Then he pulled a white envelope from the rack on the wall where Mum and Dad kept important letters. The rack was packed tight, and several other envelopes followed, landing on the counter.

Darren smiled as he ran a fingertip across the raised City crest on the reverse of the envelope in his hand. He slid the letter free, remembering how excited everybody had been when he'd read it aloud that morning, even his sisters. He'd been excited, too, of course, and still was, although now he'd had a chance to think about it he was also beginning to feel pretty nervous.

He'd always thought he was a half-decent footballer, and he supposed getting into the City FC youth squad must prove something. But what if he'd only just scraped in? The other players at the trial had been very talented, and a few had been much better than that – they'd been absolutely terrific. Darren wondered if he'd be able to cope . . . and then his toast popped up.

He spread a thin layer of Flora on both slices, because Mum and Dad had said it was important to economize everywhere, and an even thinner layer of Marmite, then ate them slowly while he read his letter yet again. Eventually, he slipped it into the envelope and gathered the others from the counter to put them back as well. But a line of red type caught his eye, and he paused.

Darren looked more carefully at the letters, realized they were bills. He peered inside the envelopes – and was horrified to see they were final demands from the phone company, the gas company, the electricity company and others, some of them very threatening about what they would do if the bills weren't paid. Darren went cold. He knew things had been difficult since Dad had stopped doing overtime, but this looked pretty bad.

Suddenly Darren heard a key in the front door, the door opening.

'Coo-ee, Darren!' his mum called out. 'Don't worry, it's only us.'

Darren swept the bills up off the counter and

hastily stuffed them back in the rack, together with his letter from City. He could hear Mum in the hall, and Gran and Grandad and the girls seemed to have arrived as well. Then he heard Dad's voice, and the kitchen door flew open and they all piled in.

'Here he is,' laughed Dad, lifting a couple of bulging Tesco bags onto the counter. Dad was tall and broad-shouldered, and everybody told Darren he looked like him, though Darren couldn't see it. Dad was still in his working clothes. 'Our very own football superstar!' he said, and squeezed Darren's shoulder.

'But . . . why aren't you and Mum at work?' Darren asked, confused, the worry caused by the bills he'd been looking at worsening. He could feel his heart beating fast in his chest, and wondered if Mum and Dad had both got the sack or been made redundant. 'You usually come home later than this,' he said. 'Is something wrong?'

'No, love,' said Mum. She was smaller than Dad, not much taller than Darren, in fact, and plump – or cuddly, as she put it. The girls were slimmer eight- and ten-year-old versions of her. 'We thought we'd have a celebration for you,' she explained, 'so we finished early and went shopping.'

'We went too, with Gran and Grandad,' said Ashleigh, the ten-year-old.

Gran and Grandad beamed happily at Darren. Gran was quite slight, with fashionably styled hair and big glasses, and Grandad was small and stocky and grey-haired. Gran started unpacking the shopping bags, Dad helping her.

'We got a chocolate cake, and some cola,' said Gemma.

'But Mum and Dad didn't have enough money,' said Ashleigh.

'So Grandad had to pay,' said Gemma, her eyes wide.

'That's OK,' said Grandad, embarrassed. 'I didn't mind.'

'And we're very grateful . . .' Mum said quickly.

Darren noticed his own dad was looking tight-lipped.

'Right,' said Gran after an awkward silence. 'Why don't you kids watch TV while we get organized? We'll let you know when every-thing's ready.'

Darren's sisters didn't have to be told twice. They skipped off into the front room and switched on the TV, but Darren didn't join them. He trudged upstairs to his room, flopped onto his bed and lay there unmoving, staring at the giant poster of Tony Adams blu-tacked to the wall above his desk.

Darren brooded. Those bills, Grandad having to pay at Tesco . . . it all made him feel very uncomfortable. Darren knew his mum and dad were under a lot of pressure because of the move two years ago. The family had needed extra space, but this house had cost a lot more than they could really afford. They hadn't even been able to decorate it properly since they'd moved in.

Mum was a council care-worker, looking after old or sick people who couldn't take care of themselves, and she didn't earn much, although Dad said she put her heart and soul into it. Dad was a delivery driver for a local company, which seemed like a pretty tough job to Darren, but he didn't earn much either. So Mum and Dad both did loads of overtime . . . until the company Dad worked for started doing badly, that is, and his overtime suddenly dried up.

Darren hated seeing his mum and dad having to work so hard anyway, and both of them getting so tired. For a long time he had secretly wished he could do something to help them.

And now he wished it more than ever.

A little while later Mum called him downstairs for his celebration dinner. It was quite a spread, too. There were hamburgers and chips, and pizza for the girls, and a chocolate fudge cake with ice cream, and plenty of cola for everybody to drink, although Dad and Grandad had a beer each instead.

'I was reading the paper after you rang us this morning, Darren,' said Grandad, 'and there was a bit in it about a young lad who went to one of these soccer academies. Can't remember his name . . . but he's sixteen now, another big club has just snapped him up, and he's getting six thousand pounds a week.'

'His name's Davy Flynn,' mumbled Dad, chasing the last few crumbs of his cake with his spoon. 'It was Rovers who signed him. I heard it as well today, on the radio in the van. And good luck to him, that's what I say.'

'There you are, Darren,' said Gran, smiling at him across the table. 'That could be you in three years. I'll bet you're just as good a player as he is.'

'And if you're going to be making that kind of money,' said Grandad, 'you can look after your gran and me in our old age. We could retire in luxury . . .'

'Hey, get to the back of the queue,' said Darren's dad. 'We're first. Don't worry, son, you just make your fortune and we'll take care of it for you.'

Everybody laughed, and Darren smiled, but he thought about what Gran had said. She was right, he was thirteen, so it *could* be him in three years. He knew top professionals made stacks of money, but to be paid that much when you were only sixteen . . . well, it would definitely solve all the family's problems, he suddenly thought. *He* would be able to pay the bills then, and that would mean Mum and Dad wouldn't have to work so hard any more.

So it was very simple: all he had to do was impress whoever it was who counted in the City FC youth squad, however tough that might actually be, and then get a big club interested enough to snap him up and pay him lots of money, just like Davy Flynn. Though he would also have to hope his mum and dad could keep going until that happened.

'Anyway,' said Mum, 'we think you've done brilliantly already, Darren, and we wanted you to know how proud of you we are. OK, everybody, I'd like to propose a toast. Here's to our Darren, and his footballing future!'

Darren sat there smiling as his family raised their glasses to him. Inside, he was steeling himself for the biggest challenge of his life.

THREE

The stadium loomed high over the surrounding streets like a massive alien spaceship that had landed among dolls' houses, Craig thought as he and his mum drove past it again, entering the colossal shadow cast by the early evening sun. Of course, Craig was familiar with the City stadium's giant, white girder framework, but the sight never failed to make his heart race. And tonight he had good reason to be excited. Or rather, two good reasons.

Not only was his mum taking him to the introductory meeting for the City youth squad, his dad was going to be there as well. Or at least Craig hoped he was, slipping a hand into his jacket pocket and crossing his fingers.

'I *still* don't see any signs for the car park,' said Mum, stopping at a red light. Craig could hear the rising tension and irritation in her voice.

Mum hated being late, and the meeting was due to start in less than ten minutes. Craig thought the prospect of spending a couple of hours with Dad probably wasn't doing a whole lot for her mood, either. When Craig had called him, Dad had immediately said he would come – much to Mum's surprise.

'And *I* still think we should go in the main entrance,' said Craig, starting to feel tense himself now about being late. 'It's the only way in for cars.'

'OK, Mr Smartypants,' said Mum as the lights changed to green. They moved off, then turned towards a large, open pair of metal gates in a high brick wall. 'Just don't blame me if this goes horribly wrong,' she added.

But it didn't. As soon as they drove through the gates, a security guard signalled for them to stop. Mum pulled over and wound down her window.

'Here for the youth squad meeting?' asked the man, smiling at them. Mum nodded. 'The car park's straight ahead, behind the Billy Watkins Stand,' he said, pointing. 'You can have any space that's not got a name on it.'

Craig smiled at his mum, and she stuck her tongue out at him. Then she thanked the guard, and they headed in the direction he had indicated, towards the stadium, which loomed ever larger, until finally it seemed to fill the sky.

Craig was fascinated. He had never seen the stadium from this side before. Whenever he'd been to a game there – and he hadn't been to as many as he would have liked – he had invariably entered through one of the turnstiles behind the South Bank. So this was all uncharted territory for him.

With its girders and open walkways, Craig thought the outside of the Billy Watkins Stand looked much like that of the South Bank, the Deepdale End, and the other main part of the stadium, the QuickPhone Stand – except for one thing. Tall glass doors stood at its centre, a giant black-and-red City crest directly above them, a semi-circle of even more imposing letters above that. 'THE CITY STADIUM – HOME OF THE HAWKS,' Craig murmured under his breath, reading the words to himself, Mum glancing at him and smiling briefly.

Mum parked at last in a long line of cars, and the two of them got out.

'Hey, there's Dad!' said Craig, spotting his father near a group of people by the glass doors.

Dad saw Craig as well, and waved. Craig ran over to him.

'Craig!' said Dad, smiling. 'Cutting it a bit fine, aren't you?'

Craig smiled back, and for a second he couldn't say anything. He hadn't seen his dad for two months, and it felt strange to be looking at the real person instead of an image in his head. Dad had dark hair and brown eyes, and was broad-shouldered. He was looking cool, too, in a black suit, a charcoal-grey shirt and a black tie, like a man who had things under control.

Craig often wondered which of his parents he resembled more, his dad or his mum, but it was pretty hard to say. Craig had light brown hair and hazel eyes, but he was almost as tall as Dad, and he was built a bit like him, too.

At any rate, that's what Craig had always told himself.

'Sorry,' said Craig. 'Mum couldn't find the car park.'

'Some things don't change, then,' said Dad, laughing and looking beyond him. Craig turned and saw Mum walking towards them, her eyes narrowed and lips tight. 'You've never had much sense of direction, have you, Karen?'

'That's a good one coming from you, Steve,' said Mum, sourly.

'I can't think what you mean,' said Craig's dad, with a teasing smile. '*I* didn't have any trouble finding it. But then we men know our way around, don't we, Craig? I suppose it must be the hunter in us, or something.'

Craig glanced at his mum, and saw her eyes narrow even more. Craig had forgotten how easily his dad could wind her up. The last thing Craig wanted was for them to start an argument. Not here, and not now, he thought. 'Shouldn't we be going in?' he said, quickly.

Luckily, just then there seemed to be some movement among the group of people standing between them and the big glass doors. Mum glanced in that direction, took a deep breath, let it out slowly, turned back to Craig. 'Yes, you're right,' she said calmly, and strode towards the entrance.

Dad grinned and winked at Craig, and the two of them followed her.

Beyond the glass doors was a large reception area, its walls covered with huge, blown-up black-and-white photographs of City players in action from every period in the club's history. Craig recognized most of them, especially one

– Joe Johnson. The picture showed him aged eighteen, scoring the extra-time goal that had won the legendary Wembley play-off game four years ago.

There was a wide counter to the side, and standing behind it was a lady receptionist with a City crest on her jacket pocket. She was talking on a phone and waving everybody through to a second set of doors, wooden this time, where another security guard was checking names against a list on a clipboard. Craig and Dad caught up with Mum as she reached him.

'Through the doors, please,' the guard said when he'd ticked their names, 'and take the stairs to the first floor. The meeting's in the conference room.'

'Sounds impressive,' said Dad, slipping his arm round Craig's shoulders as they climbed the stairs, Craig catching a whiff of his dad's distinctive scent, a mixture of cigarettes and aftershave. 'I'm glad I put my new suit on now.'

Craig smiled. That was exactly the kind of thing he wanted to hear his dad saying. He wanted him to be impressed, to think this was important.

'I'm amazed you can afford one,' said Mum, turning to look Craig's dad up and down.

'According to your solicitor you don't have a penny to spare.'

'He's right, but this is a business expense,' said Dad, fingering his lapel. 'You know how it is in my line of work, Karen. You've got to look the part.'

'What *are* you doing at the moment, Steve?' Craig's mum asked.

They had arrived at a wide landing, and yet another set of doors. Two men in club blazers with City crests stood there, one on either side. They were smiling and saying good evening, handing everybody a glossy brochure. Filing between them were the people in front of Craig and his mum and dad.

'Oh, just the usual,' said Craig's dad, vaguely. 'A bit of this, a bit of that. Although I don't mind admitting business has been pretty slow this year. Still, you'll be all right for pocket money from now on, won't you, Craig?'

'Will I?' said Craig, who hadn't been listening properly. He'd realized some of the people ahead of him were boys of his own age, and he had been studying them closely. They were the other lads who'd made it into the youth squad. He nodded at a black boy he remembered from the trial.

'Well, as far as I can make out, there's plenty of

money sloshing about in football these days,' said Dad. 'So there must be some in this for you, son.'

'Not yet, there isn't,' snapped Mum. 'As far as I know, Craig can't be paid a penny until he's at least sixteen, and then only if he gets taken on properly.'

Craig glanced at his dad, who had gone quiet, and was looking at Craig's mum as if he was digesting what she'd said. Dad opened his mouth to speak, but suddenly a mobile started ringing. Dad closed his mouth, reached into the side pocket of his suit jacket and pulled out a small, expensive-looking phone. He held it to his ear. Craig saw several people in the queue staring at them.

'Hello?' said Dad, taking his arm from Craig's shoulders and moving away to the far corner of the landing. Craig couldn't hear what else his dad said, but the conversation was short, and Dad soon returned to where Mum and Craig were waiting. Craig noticed he was frowning slightly now. 'Sorry, son, got to love you and leave you,' his dad said. 'Duty calls, I'm afraid.'

'But, Dad . . .' said Craig, glimpsing the last few people going in.

'Listen, son, why don't you phone me later and tell me all about it?' said his dad, smiling again now and giving Craig's shoulder a brief squeeze. 'It's been good to see you, though . . . and you too, Karen.' Mum didn't reply. Then Craig's dad trotted down the stairs without a backward glance.

'Come on, Craig,' said Mum gently. 'I think it's about to start.'

Craig swallowed his disappointment, went through the doors.

FOUR

'Right, I think that's everybody,' said the man behind the lectern, glancing round the room. With his shiny bald pate, his glasses on the tip of his nose, and his grey suit, he seemed like a headmaster holding assembly, Darren thought. The buzz of conversation settled as the last few people found empty seats and sat down. 'So, to coin a phrase . . .' the man said, 'let's kick off.'

There were several groans at the awful pun, but most of the audience laughed. Darren joined in, nervously. He was sitting near the front, between his dad and grandad, and trying hard not to look stupid. Mum hadn't been able to come with them because she'd been offered some extra work at the last minute, and Gran had volunteered to babysit Ashleigh and Gemma.

Darren had never been to a football stadium

before, and the outside had been impressive, to say the least. This room was impressive too, even if it was smaller than the hall at Darren's school. Along one side there were huge windows looking out onto the dark interior of the stadium, the shadow of the Billy Watkins Stand creeping across the immaculate pitch as the sun set.

The wall facing the windows was blank, but at the near end of the room there was a bar with beer pumps and bottles on glass shelves behind it, and at the far end a bank of video machines with a large screen above them. And in the centre were several neat rows of plastic chairs, most of them occupied now by the people who had just come up the stairs and into the room.

Darren and his dad and grandad had got there early, so he had been able to study the others as they'd arrived. There were twenty or so boys, and thirty-odd adults, mostly dads, he thought, with a few mums and grandparents. Some boys were in school uniform, but lots were wearing tracksuits, T-shirts and trainers, like Darren. Several were even wearing replica City shirts.

'Good evening, everybody,' said the man behind the lectern. 'My name is Roy Newton, I'm in charge of City FC's youth policy, and I'd very much like to welcome you all to the club, especially you lads. I'm sure you'll have a great time in the City youth squad, and this evening I'll be outlining what's in store for you, with a little help from some of my friends, that is . . .' Roy Newton nodded in the direction of a table to his left, where three other men sat opposite the first row of chairs. They nodded back and smiled.

'Recognize them, Darren?' whispered his dad, grinning, and nudging him in the side. 'Looks like they've wheeled out the big guns for you tonight.'

Darren *did* recognize them. The sandy-haired man was Mr Shepherd, who had been in charge of the trial at Hawks' Nest, the City training ground. But Darren had only seen the others on TV. The dark, hard-looking man in the expensive suit was Mike Wilmot, City's manager. And the young, brown-haired man in the even more expensive suit was none other than Joe Johnson.

Roy Newton continued, but for a moment Darren could barely take his eyes off Mike Wilmot and Joe Johnson. Darren had never been that close to anybody famous, and it gave him a strange feeling. This really was the big time, he thought, his nervousness suddenly increasing. Then Dad nudged him again, and Darren tried to concentrate on what Roy Newton was saying.

He started by describing the national youth

policy, then going over the City youth squad's history. He explained that the squad was divided into juniors, under-12s, under-14s, under-17s and under-19s, and apologized to anyone who'd heard all this before, Darren realizing some of the boys in the audience tonight had probably come through the juniors and the under-12s already.

Then Mr Newton talked about some of the squad's best-known graduates – Joe Johnson, and a couple of others on the fringes of the first-team squad – and QuickPhone, the club's main sponsors, who were providing most of the funding for the youth squad. Finally he handed over to Mr Shepherd.

'Thanks, Roy,' said Jimmy, swapping places with Roy Newton at the lectern. 'My name's Jimmy Shepherd, and my title isn't quite as grand as Roy's.' He paused, and smiled at Roy Newton, who shrugged and smiled back. 'I'm the Youth Coach,' he continued, 'which means I'm the one who has to go out and run around in the cold and the rain . . .'

Darren leaned forward and listened closely as Jimmy Shepherd talked. After all, this was the important stuff, this was what he would actually be doing. Evening sessions twice a week at Hawks' Nest, each one two hours long, with specialist coaches, work on fitness and skills, plus residential courses and games against other youth squads throughout the season.

Darren shrank into his seat when he heard the list of fixtures arranged for the coming season. There would be games against Rovers, City's local rivals, other Premiership sides, and against first and second division sides like Darbridge, Barnham, Cheriton. Now Darren definitely felt *very* daunted. He looked round at the other boys who were sitting there. They had all seemed pretty good to him at the trial. So what the heck would the players in the big-name, Premiership club youth squads be like?

After a while, Jimmy Shepherd asked for the blinds to be lowered so a video could be shown on the large screen behind the lectern. There were interviews with some of last year's intake, shots of training at Hawks' Nest, film of some of the games. Darren thought the pace and level of skill seemed incredible, to say the least. He sat back and wondered if he'd ever match up.

Then the blinds were raised and Mike Wilmot spoke, mostly about how vital it was to the club's future to develop young talent. And finally, Joe Johnson stood at the lectern and told them – with lots of funny stories – what he felt being in the youth squad had done for him, and how he was hoping to be at some of the under-14 sessions during the season to help Jimmy out.

'Right,' said Roy Newton eventually. 'I'll be seeing each of the lads individually over the next few weeks. But are there any questions now?'

There were plenty, as it turned out: questions from parents about whether the boys could still play for their schools or their Sunday league teams now they were involved with the City youth squad; about whether they could expect to get paid anything by City; about whether the club had a policy on racism. The answers to the first two were no, and to the third, a firm yes.

Darren's ears pricked up when he heard the question about money. He noticed the whole audience seemed to listen intently to the answer, too. At sixteen, boys the club thought had the potential to be professionals were taken on as trainees, said Roy Newton, which meant they got paid, although not much. Unless you were lucky enough to be Davy Flynn, thought Darren . . . But as far as Darren was concerned, the two most interesting questions came last.

'Are the games part of a competition?' said a dad sitting directly behind him. 'I mean, is there a proper youth squad league, or something?'

'Not as such,' said Jimmy Shepherd. 'In general we think it's best for boys of this age to play without too much pressure to compete, so regular games will be friendlies.'

Darren's spirits lightened. That didn't sound too bad.

But Jimmy Shepherd hadn't finished. 'This season, however, there will also be an under-fourteens cup, which we've entered – and that *will* be competitive.'

Darren's spirits sank – and what he heard next made them sink further.

'Especially since it's possible the final might be held as a curtain-raiser to a Premiership or cup game . . .' said Roy Newton. There was a definite buzz of interest when the audience heard that, Darren noticed. 'Although the actual decision hasn't been made yet about exactly when or where that might be,' Mr Newton added. 'Anyway, I think we have time for one *final* question.'

There was more laughter, and a few more groans. Then another dad spoke. 'I saw in a newspaper that the failure rate at most youth squads isn't far off ninety-eight per cent,' he said. 'Is that true? And what's the failure rate here at City?'

'We don't use the word *failure* at City,' said Jimmy Shepherd. 'It depends how you define it, anyway. Most of our boys enjoy their time with us, and we try to ensure that they all learn something about themselves while they're here. Some of them do go on to bigger things. Not many, it's true, but . . .'

Darren noticed the audience suddenly seemed to be listening even more intently now. He wasn't surprised. If that figure was right, succeeding in the City youth squad might be practically impossible. But he *had* to do it, he thought. If only he could think of something that might make it easier . . .

'Don't look so worried, Darren,' whispered Grandad, and patted his arm. 'You'll be fine. I bet it'll be like when I was in the army. You just need to make a friend, and then whatever happens, at least you'll be in it together.'

Darren glanced at his grandad. That wasn't a bad idea, he thought, remembering the boy who'd nodded hello on the landing outside earlier.

In fact, it wasn't a bad idea at all.

FIVE

It took Craig a day to get over his disappointment, and three more to track his father down again. Craig didn't have Dad's mobile number, so he had to keep calling the only number he had, the one at the flat where his dad had been living recently. But there was no answer – until the following Sunday night.

Craig dialled the number, and his dad answered on the second ring.

'Is that you, Dad?' Craig asked, relieved, but hardly daring to believe he'd heard his dad's voice at last. 'I've been trying to get hold of you for days.'

'Sorry, son, I was busy,' said Dad. 'You know, ducking and diving, a man's gotta do what a man's gotta do, all that. How are things, then?'

'OK,' said Craig, glancing round. His mum had come into the hall and was listening. 'You said you wanted me to tell you about the meeting,' he went on.

'Oh, right,' Dad murmured, not sounding very interested. Craig could hear the soft undertone of a TV in the background. 'You'd better fire away . . .'

Craig gabbled through what had been said at City, Dad saying 'Yeah?' or 'Right' occasionally. Craig realized Dad wasn't giving him his full attention. 'Anyway, said Craig at last, taking a deep breath and crossing his fingers by his side, where Mum couldn't see, 'I thought it'd be great if you could come to the first training session. It's this Tuesday, it's only two hours . . .'

'I don't know, son,' Dad mumbled, Craig finding it quite hard to hear him properly against the surging sound of a TV audience laughing at something a gameshow host had just said. 'I've got a lot on at the moment.'

'Could I have a word with your father, Craig?' Mum asked suddenly. She was standing next to Craig, holding her hand out for the phone. Craig gave it to her. 'Be a sweetheart and put the kettle on while I talk to him,' she said.

Craig headed for the kitchen. He filled the kettle and spooned coffee into a cup. Mum liked her coffee strong and black – and she also liked giving Dad a hard time whenever she could, Craig thought. He hoped there wasn't going to be an argument, one of those rows where she just ranted on and on at his dad. They always ended with Dad simply hanging up on her. Craig wanted another try at persuading him to come to the training session on Tuesday.

Then Craig heard his mum putting the phone down. He ran into the hall. 'Mum!' he moaned at her. 'I hadn't finished talking to him yet.'

'Don't worry, love,' she said, smiling stiffly. 'He'll come for you this Tuesday at six sharp . . . *If* he knows what's good for him,' she muttered.

For a moment Craig wondered how Mum had done it – then he decided he didn't really care. His dad would be there, and that's all that counted . . .

But on Tuesday, Dad was late. Craig kept looking out of the front-room window into the street below, and by quarter past six he was beginning to worry that his dad wasn't coming after all. Mum had just picked up the phone, her face grim, when Craig saw a dark-green, four-wheel-drive Frontera parking in the street outside their block, his dad in the driving seat.

'He's here, Mum,' Craig yelled happily, rushing into the hall and grabbing his kitbag. 'I'd better be off,' he added. But then he paused by the front door and looked back at his mum. Suddenly he felt awkward, even guilty. 'You don't really mind not coming tonight, do you?' he said. 'I mean . . .'

'Go on, you don't want to be late for your first session,' said Mum, smiling at him, even though he could tell she wasn't particularly happy. 'Have you got that letter to give to Mr Shepherd – you know, the agreement?' Craig held up the envelope containing the copy of the letter from City Mum had signed, the one that set out the rules and conditions Craig and the club had to stick to. 'OK,' she said. 'Well, good luck. I'll be thinking about you.'

Craig stuffed the envelope in the pocket of his hoodie – worn over the new tracksuit his mum had bought him, his trainers new too – and dashed out. He ran downstairs, and soon he was opening the Frontera's front passenger door.

'All right, son?' said Dad, turning his Ray-Bans in Craig's direction.

'Hey, nice wheels, or what?' said Craig, sliding onto the passenger seat and putting on his seat belt. The Frontera looked terrific. Roof rails, spare on the back, black interior, expensive CD player. 'When did you get it, Dad?'

'Oh, it's not mine,' Dad said quickly. Craig noticed him glance up at the window of the flat, where Mum was peering down at them. Even from this distance, Craig could see she was frowning. 'I'm, er . . . looking after it for an old mate,' Dad added. 'Now, where is this place you're dragging me to?'

Craig showed Dad the map in the glossy City youth squad brochure he'd been given at the introductory meeting, and they set off. Hawks' Nest wasn't that far away, about half an hour's ride through the suburbs and into the country-side. Craig chattered as they drove, but Dad didn't do much talking.

'What kind of system do you think they'll teach us, Dad?' Craig asked at last, trying to get some kind of response from his father. 'I mean, the City first team mostly plays a back four, three across the middle, one in the hole and a striking pair up front, which would be OK with me . . .'

'I haven't got the foggiest idea, Craig,' murmured Dad, slowing down to turn right. 'It's all Greek to me. To be honest, I've never really been that interested in football . . . Anyway, it looks like we've arrived. And I'll bet I managed to get you here a lot quicker than your mum did too, eh?'

Craig didn't reply, peering through the wind-screen instead. They were driving along a narrow country road between hedges, and just ahead of them was the small sign Craig remembered, the one saying: HAWKS' NEST – CITY FC. Beyond that was a pair of open gates, and Dad drove between them.

They stopped in a car park, and both got out. There were quite a few cars parked there already, and small groups of boys and men Craig recognized from the meeting were standing around in the twilight, the sun setting behind a long, low building facing them, two freshly mown pitches beyond that.

Most of the boys seemed nervous, although a few were making a point of trying to look cool. Some of the dads seemed nervous as well, a couple giving their sons hurried last-minute advice which the boys concerned were plainly doing their best to ignore, and several just looked pleased and proud.

Craig noticed the usual checking out, the boys glancing at each other, wondering about the competition. The dads were doing it too. Craig spotted several run their eyes over the Frontera and Dad. But that was OK, Craig thought. The car looked good, as did Dad in his shades and leather jacket.

Even so, Craig was worried now as he stood there with his dad – although not particularly by what the next couple of hours might hold in store. He was a lot more concerned about what Dad had just said in the Frontera. It hadn't occurred to him that his dad might not actually like football. That *was* a blow.

True, Craig didn't recall ever kicking a ball with his dad, or talking to him about City. Dad hadn't been around much before the divorce, and Craig had certainly seen a great deal less of him after it. And when Craig had gone to see City play, it had been with a friend from school, and the friend's dad.

If Dad *really* didn't like football, Craig thought, it would probably be much harder to get him to come to the training sessions and matches than he had imagined. Craig sneaked a quick peek at him, saw a bored expression on his father's face, and realized he badly needed something to get Dad interested.

But at that precise moment Craig was also badly lacking in inspiration.

'So what happens now?' said his dad eventually, looking at his watch.

'I don't know, Dad . . .' said Craig. 'Hang on, there's Mr Shepherd.'

A tracksuited Jimmy Shepherd came out of the long building and called everybody over. The scattered groups of men and boys gathered round him. 'Could I have the lads in the pavilion to get changed, please?' he said. 'I'll show you where to go, then I'll have a word with the dads.'

Craig looked at his dad, who shrugged and took a pack of cigarettes from his jacket pocket. Dad put one in his mouth, lit it with a lighter. Craig joined the boys heading into the building – the pavilion – past Jimmy Shepherd.

'Hey, I know you, don't I?' said a boy to another lad in front of Craig. 'We were at the same primary school,' the boy continued. 'You're Wayne, Davy Flynn's brother. I saw him on the news. Is he really getting paid that much?'

'Yeah, I was at Sunny Bank,' said Wayne Flynn, turning and grinning at the boy who'd spoken. 'But you don't want to believe everything you hear on TV, pal. They got it wrong. Davy's getting a whole lot more than they said.'

'You're having a laugh, aren't you?', said the boy, sounding sceptical.

'Listen, mate,' said Wayne. 'I never joke where money is concerned.'

Craig followed the pair of them through the door, earwigging furiously, suddenly believing he might just have found the solution to his problem.

Maybe this was something Dad might want to hear about, he thought . . .

SIX

Darren went into the changing room and put his kitbag on the low wooden bench running round the shiny red- and black-tiled walls. There was a line of chrome pegs above the bench, and the other boys were taking their jackets off and hanging them up, so Darren did too.

Mr Shepherd was standing near the doorway, in front of a large whiteboard with a defensive plan sketched on it. 'OK, lads, if you could all give me those letters of agreement, properly signed, I hope . . .' he said. The boys did as he asked, Mr Shepherd collecting the letters and putting them in a file. 'Right,' he said at last. 'Now, rule one – we aim to start sessions promptly at seven, which means I want you all changed and outside in no more than five minutes. Got that? Good.'

He turned and left the room, and Darren quickly began removing his clothes. He'd felt nervous in the van with his dad, but now the butterflies in his stomach seemed to be driving vans of their own. Most of the other boys were hurrying too, but some on the opposite side of the changing room were taking their time and talking. Darren listened to their banter while he put on his kit, and the new boots Gran and Grandad had bought him on Saturday.

It was the usual changing-room stuff, mostly insults, taunts and bragging, the kind of thing Darren stayed out of. The loudest voice belonged to a boy called Wayne, who had blond hair, a brace and a high opinion of himself.

'He's Davy Flynn's brother, if you're wondering,' whispered the person sitting beside Darren. 'You know, the six-grand-a-week sixteen-year-old. I don't think I want Wayne's autograph yet, though. My name's Craig, by the way.'

Darren studied Wayne Flynn closely. He'd heard a lot more about Davy Flynn in the few days since his grandad had mentioned him. Now here Darren was, sitting in the same changing room as Davy Flynn's brother, and all he could think was how ordinary Wayne looked. And how stupid he sounded.

'Mine's Darren,' said Darren, suddenly realizing Craig was the boy who'd nodded hello at the introductory meeting. 'He's got a big mouth, hasn't he?'

'He needs it to keep all that metal in,' said Craig, and smiled. 'Ready?'

'Just about,' said Darren, smiling back, and they made for the door, their studs clattering on the concrete floor. Darren caught sight of Wayne's flashy red boots as they passed him, and thought they probably cost at least three times as much as his own. Craig rolled his eyes at them, and Darren smiled.

Jimmy Shepherd was waiting on the touchline of the near pitch. He was holding a clipboard now, and two other men in tracksuits were standing behind him, one tall and fair-haired, the other shorter, dark and sporting a moustache. Most of the dads were in a huddle nearby, and Darren noticed several were looking grumpy, although his own dad seemed happy enough.

The sun had gone down, and the floodlights had been put on. Darren hadn't registered them before. They were at the top of tall poles spaced out round both pitches, and gave each boy a ring of linked shadows. There was that early season, autumnal chill in the air too, and a strong smell of newly cut grass. A squad of older boys – probably the under-17s, Darren thought – was on the far pitch already, a couple of coaches yelling instructions at them.

Darren and Craig had been the first of the under-14s to emerge from the pavilion, but the rest soon followed, Wayne Flynn bringing up the rear. He was the only one who appeared to be sure of himself, although a better word for Wayne's expression would have been cocky, thought Darren. The rest were all looking uncertain or nervous, and no-one was saying much.

'Right lads, gather round, please,' said Jimmy Shepherd. 'Now before we get started tonight, there are a couple more rules you ought to know about. I've already told your dads there's to be no coaching or abuse from them . . .'

So that's why some of the dads were cheesed off, thought Darren. A lot of dads got very wound up when they watched their sons playing – Darren had seen plenty behaving as if a game involving ten-year-olds was a World Cup Final, yelling instructions at their sons and abuse at the opposition, swearing at the referee, arguing with each other, almost getting into fights sometimes. His own dad got excited watching him, but never like that, thank goodness.

The main rules for the boys were simple. No

unexplained absences from training, no swearing, no racist remarks, and the most important rule of all – the gaffer's word was always law, and Jimmy Shepherd was . . . the gaffer. That's what he liked to be called. That, or 'boss'.

'But what if someone doesn't agree with you, er . . . *sir*?' said Wayne in his loud voice, flicking his fringe out of his eyes and smirking at the others.

'Then he won't last long at City, son,' replied Jimmy Shepherd, quietly. 'And that reminds me of another important rule . . . no backchat. OK?'

Wayne's smirk faded and became a sulk, but Jimmy Shepherd just moved on to ticking off their names, and outlining what the session would involve. A warm-up first, then some basic skills work with the other two men – who turned out to be assistant coaches, the tall one called Des, the one with the moustache, Andy – then a short practice game, and a warm-down to finish.

The warm-up was fairly easy. They started with a gentle jog round the pitches, then did some stretching, then more jogging with jumping and turning, then more stretches. Darren remembered watching the build-up to games on

TV and seeing professionals going through a similar routine.

Darren and Craig stuck together right through the warm-up, so naturally they did the same when Jimmy Shepherd told the boys to divide into pairs. Des fetched a net bag full of balls and distributed one to every pair, then Andy got each boy to stand three or four metres away from his partner.

'Right, we'll start with the real basics,' said Jimmy Shepherd. 'I just want to see you passing and controlling the ball. Two touches, control and pass . . .'

They did that for ten minutes, then he got them to vary it. Control and pass with alternate feet, control, flick up and volley back, control and chip for a headed return. And all the time Jimmy Shepherd was walking round the pairs of boys, watching, commenting, making notes . . .

Darren felt those butterflies in his stomach driving more wildly now. It was obvious what Mr Shepherd was doing, he thought. Mr Shepherd – Darren tried to think of him as the gaffer, but the name felt strange as yet – was checking them out, seeing where their strengths and weaknesses lay.

That's what this whole first session was about,

thought Darren as he controlled a chip from Craig on his chest, let it bounce and half-volleyed it back. But he was doing OK, Darren told himself. He didn't make any mistakes, not even when Mr Shepherd stood and watched him closely.

It helped that Craig was such a good partner. Darren glimpsed pairs where one partner was trying to be way too clever, or hit difficult balls for the other so he'd look useless, Wayne being the worst offender, of course. But like Darren, Craig was concentrating on doing the drill properly. Grandad had been dead right, thought Darren. Having a friend did make a difference.

By the time they'd gone through a lot more drills – running with the ball, passing and turning, passing and tackling two on two, then three on two – the butterflies in Darren's stomach were definitely slowing down. None of what he'd been asked to do so far was as tough as he'd thought it might be.

'Right, gather round again, lads,' said Mr Shepherd at last. 'You can take a breather for a few minutes, then we'll have that game I promised you.'

'This is well good, isn't it?' said Craig, grinning and passing Darren the water bottle he'd been given by Andy. Darren nodded, and squirted water down his throat. 'Anyway,' said Craig, 'I'm a striker. What about you?'

'Central defender,' said Darren. 'Hope we're on the same side.'

But when Mr Shepherd read out the two teams from his clipboard, Darren and Craig discovered they were opponents. Des and Andy distributed two sets of coloured bibs, one set red and the other yellow. Jimmy Shepherd told the boys he'd ref, and that they were to take it easy and enjoy themselves.

And Darren did feel almost relaxed as he took up his position in defence for the red team. He nodded to his fellow defenders and the keeper, and waited for the kick-off. He glanced up-field, and saw Craig standing next to another yellow-bibbed striker, the ball on the centre spot between them.

Mr Shepherd blew his whistle. The ball was tapped to Craig, who moved forward. Craig beat one red player, a second, a third, and accelerated away from a chaser. Darren was startled by his pace, and quickly stepped up to close him down, thinking his fellow defenders would cover the gap he'd left.

But they didn't. Craig kept on coming, Darren shaped to challenge him, Craig pulled a Cruyff turn, Darren lunged, missed and fell. He could only watch as Craig rounded the keeper and stroked the ball into the net.

Darren suddenly wished the pitch would open up and swallow him.

SEVEN

Usually when Craig scored a goal as good as that he'd celebrate like the top players he'd seen on TV, running with his arms out-stretched as if they were wings and even, sometimes, pulling his shirt up over his head, or heading for the corner flag to do his special victory dance. But he didn't know whether the gaffer would approve, so he simply turned and jogged back into his own half.

Still, it was great to start with a goal, he thought, and it *had* been a good one, too. Craig couldn't help grinning, especially when he heard a scatter of applause from the fathers on the touchline, and somebody calling out, 'Great goal!' Craig glanced in their direction, but most of them were in the shadows between the flood-light poles, and he couldn't tell if it had been his own dad.

Then Craig glimpsed a flare inside a parked car, and saw it was his dad in the Frontera, lighting a cigarette. Craig realized the Frontera was actually facing away from the red team's half, so his dad wasn't even looking at the pitch. Which must mean he'd missed the goal, Craig thought, his pleasure in it slowly seeping out of him like the air from a balloon being let down.

'Not bad, I suppose,' said a loud voice behind him. Craig turned and saw Wayne Flynn smirking, hands on hips. Wayne was playing central midfield for the reds. 'Mind you, it had to be a fluke, didn't it?' said Wayne, hawking loudly and gobbing onto the turf very close to Craig's left boot. Then Wayne ambled over, stood directly in front of Craig, stared him right in the eyes. 'And I bet you couldn't do it again, pal,' he said. 'Bet you anything you like.'

Craig paused. Several other lads nearby had heard Wayne's words, and they must have understood the challenge in them, Craig thought. *He* had. He knew that if he didn't score again this evening, and do it just as well, then Wayne would claim he had been proved correct, that the goal *had* been a fluke. And Craig couldn't allow Wayne to get away with that, not this early on in Craig's career at City FC. It would definitely give Wayne the edge.

Craig glanced upfield and saw Darren standing alone, looking sheepish. Craig liked Darren, and thought he could turn out to be a real mate, so he hadn't enjoyed showing him up in front of everyone. But there could never be any favours or friendships in football, Craig decided, not once the whistle went. Darren would just have to look after himself on the pitch.

Besides, thought Craig, next time he scored, his dad might be on the touchline . . .

'Oh yeah?' he said, running into the centre circle. 'Watch me . . . *pal*.'

Wayne laughed, doing his best to show everybody he was unimpressed. But Craig knew he'd shown the rest of the squad he wasn't to be messed with. Although he'd have to follow through, let his actions speak for him.

'Well taken, son,' said Jimmy Shepherd, smiling at Craig once both teams were back in position for the re-start. 'And let that be a lesson to the rest of you,' he added, raising his voice. 'You need to concentrate right from the kick-off, every time, otherwise you'll be in trouble. Got that, red defence?'

Craig saw Darren nod unhappily, then the

gaffer blew his whistle, and reds kicked off. Most of the lads were wary now, not wanting to do anything stupid or let themselves be shown up, as Darren had been. So for the next few minutes it was all very tentative. But eventually some of the braver souls started trying to turn it on, with a curled pass here, a neat chip there.

The tempo soon increased, even though Jimmy Shepherd froze the game a couple of times, blowing his whistle and getting them to stand still where they were so he could make points about their positioning. Craig thought the gaffer was brilliant at explaining that kind of stuff, and suddenly he started to feel happy again. He almost pinched himself to see if he was dreaming after all.

He scored his second goal a few moments later.

Wayne knocked a long ball out to his right wing-back, a skilful, gangly red-head Craig had heard some of the others call Jamie. But Wayne had put too much pace on the pass, Jamie didn't manage to get a good first touch, and the yellow team's left full-back – a serious-looking black kid called Paul – closed him down almost immediately, Jamie quickly losing possession.

The ball ran to a yellow-bibbed midfielder whose name Craig hadn't yet learned, a stocky, dark-haired boy who seemed to know what he was doing. The midfielder brought it quickly upfield, and Craig came back towards him, calling for the ball, suddenly aware of a red team defender breathing down his own neck. Then the midfielder drilled a hard, low pass through to Craig's feet. Craig controlled it, carefully shielding the ball from his marker.

Craig had taken it easy since that opening surprise, making only a couple of runs into space, keeping fairly quiet, generally lulling the opposition into a false sense of security, allowing them to believe that maybe Wayne had got his measure. But now, as Craig stood there facing downfield towards his half with the ball at his feet, he suddenly knew it was time to rock and roll.

He dummied to his left, then hooked the ball with the outside of his boot to the right, spun the defender, burst away. The defender lost his balance and went down, but Craig ignored him and moved quickly on the opposition box, looking to see how many more defenders blocked his path to their goal.

The sky was deep black now, the pitch an island of harsh white light surrounded by darkness. Craig could hear his breathing as he ran, the rhythmic tap-tap-tap of his boot on the ball as he dribbled, and somebody shouting behind him. But the words were muffled, distant, unimportant.

There were three defenders ahead, the keeper behind them on the edge of the six-yard box. Darren was in the middle, hanging off, waiting to see what Craig might do. The left full-back – a hard-looking boy with a buzz-cut – was nicely positioned in line with Darren. Craig knew he could tackle, too.

But the other defender – a big lad with curly black hair – had moved out to cover Jamie's run upfield, and was only now scrambling back. So there was a wide gap between him and Darren . . . Craig instantly decided to exploit it, suddenly changing the angle of his approach and slowing down slightly.

Craig wanted to tempt Darren towards him, and took another touch, pushing the ball just far enough ahead to give Darren the feeling he might have a chance of reaching it first. Craig knew Darren would only get a split second to decide . . . then Darren did exactly what he was hoping for.

Darren lunged forward to make the tackle. But Craig just lengthened his stride, slid the ball under Darren's flailing boot, hurdled his legs, collected the ball again, and was suddenly clear, the box in front of him, the keeper quickly coming out to narrow the angle, the left full-back racing to cover the line.

But it was too late. Craig beat them both with a shot that whipped round the keeper, the ball dipping into the top right-hand corner and billowing the net. Craig turned, and saw Darren getting to his feet, looking even more crestfallen than before. Craig ran past him without saying anything.

He did allow himself a modest celebration this time, though, raising his arm in acknowledgement of the renewed applause from the touchline, just in case his father might be there. Craig glanced at Wayne, and was surprised to see a strange look on his face, an expression that could almost have been envy.

The rest of the game flew past, nobody else scoring again for either side. Des and Andy took them through the warm-down, and that was it, the session was over. The gaffer stood by the pavilion doors as the boys filed in, most of them laughing now, relaxed and relieved they'd got through the evening.

'Well done, lads,' said the gaffer. 'Good session, you worked hard, and that's what being a pro is all about. Nice goals, er . . . Craig, isn't it?' Craig nodded and smiled. 'Might do a few defensive drills on Thursday, though,' Jimmy Shepherd added, looking at Darren, 'make it a bit harder for you.'

Craig glanced at Darren, who was blushing and keeping his head down. But Craig was too happy with the way his evening had gone to worry about anybody else. Soon he was hurrying outside to the car park with its revving engines and dazzling headlights. He found the Frontera and climbed in.

'What did you think, then, Dad?' he asked. 'Mr Shepherd said . . .'

'I think . . . that's a *very* nice motor,' said his dad quietly, peering ahead.

Craig followed his gaze through the windscreen as they moved off, and realized Dad was talking about the Cherokee in front. The Frontera's lights showed Wayne Flynn sitting in the front passenger seat. So the Cherokee's driver – who was wearing a baseball cap and seemed to be talking rather than looking where he was going – must be Wayne's dad, Craig thought.

'Well, they've just struck it rich,' said Craig, wanting to impress his dad with something, anything connected to City and football, however vaguely.

'Really?' said Dad, suddenly sounding interested. 'How come?'

Craig smiled, then told him as they drove through the darkness.

EIGHT

It was hard to believe things could have gone so badly wrong, Darren thought bitterly as he took his jacket from the peg and pulled it on. He carelessly stuffed his dirty boots and kit in his bag, angrily zipped it shut, grabbed the handles, then trudged out of the changing room with his head down, unable to look any of the lads in the eye. He was glad Craig hadn't hung around.

Darren walked past the gym and the physio suite, ignoring the older boys and coaches who were in both. He headed for the car park, desperate to get away – and almost stopped dead in his tracks when he saw Jimmy Shepherd talking to a couple of dads near the door. Darren swallowed nervously, and tried to walk round them, hoping he wouldn't be noticed. But he was.

'Hold on a second, son,' said Jimmy Shepherd. 'I'd like a word.'

Darren had to wait while Mr Shepherd finished his conversation with the dads. Darren's stomach had suddenly started churning with worry, and he wondered if this was it already, if he was going to be dropped from the City youth squad after his very first training session. It would probably be a world record, he thought. The fastest failure in the history of youth football.

Eventually the dads left, and the gaffer turned to Darren, who swallowed nervously, waiting for his doom to be pronounced.

Then the gaffer smiled. 'There's no need to look so miserable, er . . . Darren, isn't it?' he said, checking the name on his clipboard. 'You did OK tonight – apart from those goals, that is. I know it's always difficult when a defence hasn't played together before . . . but Craig still suckered you there, didn't he?'

'I suppose so,' said Darren as a couple of boys slipped by, staring. He could feel warmth spreading on his cheeks, and knew that he was blushing.

'Well, don't worry about it,' said Jimmy Shepherd. 'Just watch out for that in future. And remember, no matter how good a striker is, he's bound to have a weakness. All you've got to do is find it . . . and make sure you time your tackles

71

right, which is something we can work on. See you Thursday, OK?'

Darren nodded, then pushed through the pavilion doors and made his way through the swiftly emptying car park towards his dad's battered van.

He got in, and soon they were driving along dark country lanes, then under streetlamps on quiet suburban streets. His dad glanced at him from time to time, asked him whether the session had been how he'd expected, what the other lads were like, if he'd picked up any knocks. Darren barely grunted in reply, his shoulders slumped, his eyes fixed on the road unrolling ahead.

'You all right, son?' his dad asked eventually. 'You're very quiet.'

'I'm fine, Dad,' said Darren, staring into the dark. 'I'm just tired.'

So his dad gave up, and they passed the rest of the journey in silence, Darren replaying over and over again in his mind the two moments when Craig had beaten him. He thought about what Mr Shepherd had said, about every striker having a weakness, no matter how good he was. But Darren thought the gaffer was wrong. Craig seemed utterly unstoppable.

Craig had also made the perfect start to his City career, Darren thought, while all *he* had done was look useless, and get spoken to by Mr Shepherd. So there must already be a question mark against the name Darren Kimble on the coach's clipboard, which was worrying . . . At school, Darren brooded, if you got off on the wrong foot with a new teacher, it could be hard to make them change their minds about you. And it was probably the same here.

And it had to be Craig who'd given him the run-around, the one person he'd made friends with. Darren wanted to hate Craig for what he'd done – but he couldn't. He knew he wouldn't have gone easy on Craig if the positions had been reversed. That was football, and Darren was sure they could still be mates. So long as he kept his place, that is, he thought . . .

It was nearly ten o'clock when they parked outside the house. Darren dumped his bag in the hall, and he and his dad hung up their jackets. Darren could hear the low murmur of the TV from the front room, and went in there, his dad going to fetch him a drink and put the kettle on. Grandad was sitting on the sofa, the room lit only by a lamp in one corner and the TV's glow.

'Hello, Darren,' said Grandad. 'Your gran's upstairs checking on the girls, which means us boys have got complete control of the TV. I was waiting for the news, then the highlights of that

European game. Anyway, how did you get on this evening? Did you amaze everybody with your incredible talent?'

'Er . . . not exactly, Grandad,' mumbled Darren as his dad came in.

'Don't listen to him, Dad,' said Darren's father, handing Darren a glass of icy cold milk. 'You did OK, Darren,' he added, smiling at his son.

Yeah, thought Darren, sitting in an armchair, that was what Mr Shepherd had said. He'd done OK – as in average, ordinary, definitely *not* brilliant.

'I'm glad,' said Grandad, turning his attention back to the TV as a familiar burst of music signalled the end of the commercials. 'Ah, here's the news.'

Darren sipped his milk, said hello to his gran when she came into the front room and sat down. The newsreader was going through the headlines for the main stories – something about a war somewhere, an argument about the economy between some politicians, a report on global warming, none of it really catching Darren's attention . . . until he heard a particular name.

'The Football Association has announced an official inquiry into the case of the six-thousand-pounds-a-week sixteen-year-old, Davy Flynn,' intoned the newsreader, 'after allegations of irregularities in his recent transfer . . .'

'That doesn't sound too good, does it?' murmured Grandad, frowning.

Darren instantly thought of Wayne, and waited impatiently while the newsreader went back to the other main stories to cover them in depth. The Flynn inquiry was the last item, right at the end of the bulletin. It seemed that Davy Flynn's previous club was making an official complaint that an agent had approached him while he'd still been registered with their youth squad, and under sixteen.

'I don't understand,' said Gran. 'Is there a rule against that, then?'

'Yeah, they were very specific about it at City, Mum,' said Darren's dad. 'Once a boy is signed up to one club's youth squad, no other league club is supposed to try and poach him. Certainly not until he's over sixteen, anyway.'

'But this was an agent, not another club,' said Gran, looking puzzled.

'It makes no difference,' said Darren's dad. 'In fact, from what they were saying at City, the rules about agents and boys under sixteen are even stricter.'

Darren concentrated on the screen while the

adults talked, his eyes fixed on film of Davy Flynn training and playing. Then there was a brief interview with the agent, a smooth, dark-suited man called John Vulpine. He said he was happy to co-operate with the FA, that he had absolutely nothing to fear from any inquiry. Darren thought he seemed very cool and confident.

'Well, if you ask me, there's no smoke without fire,' said Grandad.

'And your mum will be breathing fire if you're not in bed by the time she gets in, Darren,' said his dad. 'Although you'd better have a bath first . . .'

Darren said good night to his grandparents, who left while he was in the bath. Half an hour later he was in bed, flicking through a copy of *Shoot!* his grandad had bought him. There was a story about Davy Flynn, but Darren didn't read it. Darren was convinced now that *he'd* never attract the attention of an agent, or get signed by a big club and paid huge amounts of money.

Just then he heard the front door open, and his mum come in, and his dad asking her if she wanted a cup of tea or anything to eat. They went into the kitchen, and Darren slipped out of bed and onto the landing. The doors of his sisters' rooms were ajar, and he could see they were both sound asleep. He crept halfway down the darkened stairs and peeked through the banisters.

The kitchen door was open. Darren saw his dad refilling the teapot, his mum sitting at the table looking exhausted, still in her coat, her uniform underneath. Darren listened to them talking for a while, mostly about bills.

'I don't know if I can keep this up,' said Mum at last. 'I'm whacked.'

'And I wish you didn't have to do it, love,' said Dad, his back to her. She couldn't see how unhappy he looked, but Darren could. 'I still can't get any overtime, though. In fact, they're even talking about laying some of us off.'

'Oh, great,' said Mum gloomily. 'Anyway, how did Darren get on?'

'He did fine,' said Dad, and smiled at her. 'He might just save us yet.'

'I can't wait,' said Mum. 'The sooner he makes that fortune, the better.'

Darren turned away, crept silently back to his room, slid under his duvet.

Even his mum and dad were beginning to believe he might be the answer to the family's problems, he thought, and he decided there and then that he couldn't let them down . . . He just *had* to succeed at City – whatever it might take.

So maybe he'd have to find that weakness in Craig after all.

NINE

Craig sat on the sofa in his tracksuit, flicking through channels with the TV remote. He paused at MTV to watch the video of a new song he liked, then found his way to a sports channel and highlights of a Real Madrid–Bayern game. The display on the TV told him it was 5.50, so he had ten minutes to kill till his dad picked him up. He was pretty certain Dad wouldn't be late.

The previous Thursday, Dad had arrived at exactly six o'clock to take him to the second training session. There had been another session on Saturday morning instead of a game – the first friendly match was scheduled for the weekend after next – and Dad hadn't been late to take him to that, either. And on Tuesday evening Dad had actually turned up a few minutes early.

'Are you sure you've had enough to eat, Craig?' said his mum, who was standing in the doorway looking at him. Mum had changed her office hours so she could make it home every Tuesday and Thursday in time to cook him a proper meal, before he had to go out. 'I know what you're like where food is concerned,' she added. 'You'll be starving by nine o'clock. There's plenty of fruit, so why don't you have a banana, or an apple, or something? I could . . .'

'I'm all right, Mum,' Craig replied, turning back to the TV. 'Besides, Dad said we can stop on the way home and have a burger if I feel hungry.'

'Huh,' snorted Mum, obviously irritated. 'That's absolutely typical of your father, encouraging you to eat greasy junk food at that time of night,' she said, coming into the room and standing over Craig, her voice sounding more cross with every syllable she spoke. 'It'll ruin your digestion – and I don't remember seeing hamburgers on that healthy diet sheet the club gave you.'

'But Dad and me *like* burgers,' muttered Craig, not taking his eyes off the screen, the resentment he'd been feeling against his mum for the last few days creeping into his voice. 'Why do you have to keep being so horrible about him, anyway?' he added, the words slipping out before he could stop them.

'I don't know what you mean,' Mum spluttered. Craig glanced at her, and noticed that she was blushing slightly. 'I don't think . . .' she started to say.

'Oh, come on, Mum, you never, *ever* have a good word to say for Dad,' said Craig bitterly, suddenly feeling pretty cross himself, deciding to let her know what he really thought. It would be better to have all this in the open. 'You just don't want him to have anything to do with me, do you?' he said.

'That's not true, Craig, and you know it,' said Mum. She sat on the sofa, but Craig turned his gaze back to the TV. 'When have I made it difficult for him to see you?' she asked. 'He could have come more if he'd wanted.'

'He *did* want to, he just couldn't,' said Craig, turning to face her. 'I asked him about it on Tuesday, and he explained. It's always been difficult for him to visit me much because he's busy, he has to see people and do deals . . .'

'Oh yes, your father and his . . . *deals*,' muttered Mum. 'So why has he got more time for you all of a sudden? I don't remember him being particularly interested in football before. And how come he can afford new suits and a new car – but he still can't provide any maintenance for you?'

'I've told you, the Frontera belongs to one of his friends,' said Craig, wearily. 'Dad's just looking after it for him. Dad explained about the suit, too, I was there, I heard him . . . and he does like football now, OK? Anyway, I don't care about the maintenance. I'm not interested in Dad's money.'

'As far as that's concerned, Craig,' snapped Mum, 'I'm afraid *your* opinion doesn't count. He's your father, and he should help to support you . . .'

'But why?' said Craig angrily. 'You make enough to pay our bills. I mean, we're not exactly starving to death, are we? Actually, I think all this stuff about money just gives you an excuse to keep having a go at him. Maybe *that's* why he hasn't been to see me more often. Have you thought of that?'

For a second Craig thought Mum might really lose her temper with him. She opened her mouth to say something . . . but then she closed it, and sighed deeply instead. Craig turned back to the TV, and mother and son sat there on the sofa, the commentator's drone filling the tense silence between them.

'Listen, Craig,' said Mum at last, in the quiet voice she used when she was trying to make friends after an argument. 'I'm only thinking of you. Believe me, I understand how important your football is, and why you want your dad to be involved. But you don't know him like I do. And I don't trust him.'

'That's not fair!' said Craig. 'He's only been late once, hasn't he?'

'It's got nothing to do with being late,' said Mum, squeezing Craig's hand. Craig crossly snatched it away. 'Believe me, love, I know how it feels to be disappointed,' she went on. 'And I'd hate to see your father let you down.'

'He won't,' snapped Craig, hearing two beeps from a car in the street. He jumped to his feet, glanced through the window, then dashed past his mum and into the hall. He grabbed his jacket and bag, yelled, 'See you later,' and went out of the door. He heard his mum calling after him, but ignored her.

His dad was waiting in the Frontera, and smiled as Craig climbed in. 'OK, son?' he said, putting the car in gear and pulling away.

'Yeah, I suppose so,' muttered Craig, clicking in his seat belt.

'You don't sound too sure,' said Dad as they turned into the main road, busy with rush-hour traffic. The sky was full of low, dark-grey, bulging clouds, and soon fat drops of rain were spattering across the Frontera's windscreen. Dad switched on his wipers and lights. 'What's up?' he said.

'Nothing,' said Craig, shrugging. 'Mum and me had a row, that's all.'

'Has she been giving you a hard time?' asked Dad, glancing at him. Craig kept his eyes on the car ahead of them, and nodded. 'What about?' said Dad.

'Er . . . not tidying my room,' said Craig, suddenly feeling uneasy.

Craig was angry with his mum, and his first instinct had been to tell his dad what she'd been saying, so Dad could prove that she was completely wrong. But what if Dad thought he had believed any of it, and got upset with *him*? No, it was all too difficult, Craig decided . . . much better simply to avoid the subject, just in case, even if it meant telling his father a fib. He didn't want to spoil things with his dad, not now they had started to go so brilliantly.

It really *was* great having his dad there at the training sessions, Craig thought. After that first time, Dad had stayed on the touchline, and judging by some of the conversations they'd had on the journeys home, he'd been watching closely. Dad also seemed to have struck up quite a friendship with Wayne Flynn's father, and had learned a bit about the game from him.

Craig didn't mind that, even though Mr Flynn could be pretty loud and opinionated, just like his son. But Craig couldn't stand Wayne at all. The more he saw of him, the more he disliked him. Not that he'd told Dad.

'That's something else that hasn't changed, then,' said Dad, and laughed. The traffic light ahead showed amber, and he accelerated to beat it. Craig saw it change to red as they shot past, but they made it over the junction. 'Typical woman, your mum, always fanatically tidy,' Dad went on. 'She was forever on at me not to make any mess. It drives you barmy, doesn't it?'

'Yeah, sometimes,' said Craig, laughing too, although now he felt slightly more uneasy. Talking like this with his dad was good, he thought; this must be how it was with most fathers and sons, males sticking together. But Craig couldn't avoid the feeling that he was also somehow being disloyal to Mum. Besides, now he came to think about it, he had always been a fairly tidy person himself. It was one of the things he and his mum had in common.

'Anyway, did you remember to bring your scrapbook?' said Dad. They were leaving the suburbs behind, and the rain was beginning to ease off.

'It's in my bag,' said Craig, and smiled, all his

uneasiness gone. After the last session, Craig had mentioned his scrapbook, and Dad had asked to see it.

The scrapbook contained certificates from football courses Craig had been on, copies of his primary school newsletter with match reports, clippings from the local paper with reports of the county games he'd played in, a certificate from his Sunday team for being their best ever scorer, with a huge number of goals in one season, more even than Michael Owen had scored at the same age. And in pride of place, of course, his letter of acceptance from City. Mum had wanted to frame it and put it on the front-room wall, but Craig was glad now he'd kept it for his scrapbook. That was exactly the right place for it.

'Terrific, I'll have a look at that later, while you're training,' said Dad, swinging the Frontera round a tight, narrow bend and overtaking another car. 'I might even want to borrow it for a few days, if that's OK with you.'

'Of course it is, Dad,' said Craig, flushing with deep pleasure, starting to look forward to an evening with Darren and the other mates he'd made.

If only Mum would realize just how wrong she was, he thought.

TEN

Darren jogged onto the near pitch and headed for the group of lads in the centre circle. The October sky was darkening, even though it wasn't seven o'clock yet, and the floodlights were already on, each one given a silver halo by the rain that had settled into a drizzle. There was a sharp wind, too, and Darren was glad his mum had made him bring his thicker tracksuit top.

'All right, Dazza?' said Paul as Darren reached the group, which opened to let him in. By now Darren had made friends with a few more boys, and most of his mates were there. It hadn't taken long for nicknames to start being handed out – Jamie, of course, was Ginge, Paul was Bandy, Drew was Big Ears – under the circumstances, Darren thought he'd got off pretty lightly.

'Yeah, fine,' said Darren, glancing round. Some of the other lads were out on the pitch too.

Jason Woods – a sly-looking boy Darren didn't like much – was standing a few metres away, talking to his two constant companions, Nicky Jones and Glen Harris. And Darren could also see Lee Powell on the touchline, his dad talking animatedly at him, Lee with a sullen expression on his face. But he couldn't see Craig. 'So where's Twink, then?' he asked.

'Over there,' said Drew, the tall defender with big ears. He turned and spat casually, then nodded towards the goal nearest the car park. 'With Motormouth. Christ knows why he wants to talk to that loser, though.'

Darren looked while the others laughed and joked, and saw Craig and Wayne together beside the goal, their dads talking to each other nearby.

Motormouth was the name the lads had chosen for Wayne, because he never seemed to stop talking. But it was Des the coach who had named Craig Twinkle Toes, after a particularly dazzling dribble during the second training session, the other lads inevitably shortening it to Twinkle, and finally Twink.

Even at this distance, and even though they weren't in the full glare of the floodlights, Darren could see that Wayne's mouth was moving, and that Craig wasn't looking too happy. But then Darren knew Craig simply couldn't stand Wayne, which wasn't much of a surprise, as most of the lads in the squad felt the same. But Craig's dad seemed to be getting on with Wayne's father like nobody's business, which must make things pretty awkward for Craig . . .

Although it hadn't affected Craig's game much, Darren thought. In the sessions since that first nightmare of an evening, he had studied Craig, searching for that weakness, but with no success so far. Craig seemed the perfect striker. He had bags of self-confidence. He had superb control, his first touch being especially excellent. He had real pace. He was great in the air. He was very strong, and couldn't be hustled off the ball – not fairly, at any rate – and he was lethal inside the area. Craig did seem a little obsessed with his father, thought Darren, but that hardly counted as a weakness.

Then, as Darren watched, Craig took a ball out of the big net bag that Andy had left near the goal. Craig rolled it back under his boot and began juggling it, from foot to foot, up to his knees, onto his head, and down to his feet again. Darren knew he could keep it off the ground for ever.

Darren refused to admit defeat, though. The gaffer had worked with him on timing his tackles, and Darren had listened carefully to his advice. In the practice games, he had shadowed Craig, only committing himself when he was covered by other defenders. Craig had still beaten him several times and scored, but at least Darren hadn't been made to look quite such a fool as before. So things were going OK, Darren thought. Not great, but OK . . .

'Here comes the gaffer,' said Jamie suddenly. 'Bang on seven o'clock.'

'Hey, I don't believe it!' said Paul. 'He's got Joe Johnson with him.'

Darren looked, and to his amazement saw that Paul was right. The gaffer was striding onto the pitch, and alongside him was the tall, track-suited, yet totally unmistakable figure of Joe Johnson, Des and Andy trotting behind them. Suddenly there was a real buzz of excitement among the lads. Darren felt it himself, although for him the thrill was laced with sudden anxiety. He wondered if this meant the session would somehow be harder now.

'Could we make a start, everybody, please?' the gaffer called out, clapping his hands. The boys came over from wherever they'd been waiting, and gathered round the four men. Craig appeared next to Darren, and the two friends nodded and smiled at each other. 'We're very lucky tonight to have a special visitor,' said the gaffer. 'I think you probably all know who this is . . .'

'I wish they didn't,' Joe Johnson muttered, 'not after last Saturday's performance, anyway. I've been thinking of changing my name, or maybe even leaving the country. What do you reckon, gaffer? Is my career over?'

For a brief instant Darren thought he was being serious, but then he saw a faint smile flickering round his lips, and realized it was a joke. He knew what Joe Johnson was talking about, though. City had begun the season poorly, with only two wins and a draw out of eight games. Saturday's match had been at home against fellow strugglers Southampton. But City had lost a scrappy contest 1–0, Joe Johnson missing a couple of real sitters.

'Probably not,' said the gaffer, smiling too. 'But think yourself lucky I'm not your coach any more. I'd have your guts for garters, wouldn't I?'

'Oh yeah,' said Joe Johnson, winking at the lads. 'And my eyeballs for gobstoppers. Anyway, are we going to do any training tonight, or what?'

'We are,' said the gaffer, 'and seeing as you're so keen, you can lead the warm-up. I think we should start with a couple of laps of the pitches . . .'

The lads groaned, but it was pretty good-natured. Darren could feel they'd all been fascinated by the exchange between Joe Johnson and the gaffer. It was like seeing an older boy who'd left your school coming back to visit a favourite teacher, and talk to a grown-up in a way you couldn't – yet. Only this older boy played in the Premiership and earned huge amounts of money.

Though it seemed none of that had made him big-headed, thought Darren. In fact, Joe Johnson was friendly and helpful to them all. After the warm-up, he joined in with the drills and exercises, giving the lads advice while he did the same as them, even doing the usual punishment of ten push-ups when he made a mistake. And he kept up a constant stream of banter throughout.

Then the gaffer told them to divide into groups for a two-on-two exercise, two attackers versus two defending a mini-goal, the whole thing played in squares marked out by cones. Darren, Craig and Paul soon got together, but before Jamie or Drew could make the fourth, Joe Johnson came over.

'Mind if I join you lads?' he said, grinning at them.

None of the three was going to argue,

although for a second Darren felt like asking if *he* could join another group. Panic rose in him as Joe Johnson lined up with Craig to make the attacking two, leaving Darren and Paul as the two defenders. Then the gaffer blew his whistle, and the exercise began.

As the gaffer had said when they'd done the exercise the first time, for attackers it was all about close control, taking on markers, using wall passes to penetrate the defence. For defenders it was about staying between the ball and the goal, being patient and aware, keeping attackers under pressure.

Darren forced the panic down and tried to concentrate. Joe Johnson was coming forward, the ball at his feet. Darren advanced to cover him, but didn't attempt a tackle, not wanting to be suckered. Joe Johnson smiled, took another touch, then knocked the ball short to Craig, who controlled it.

Paul closed in on Craig, jockeying him towards the cones at the edge of the square, Craig finally having to pass back to Joe Johnson . . . And that's how things went for a while, Paul and Darren working well together, Joe Johnson and Craig seemingly unable to find a way through them to score.

Darren began to feel less worried. Nobody

was going to blame him or Paul if an adult professional ran them ragged, he realized – they were only thirteen, after all. Not that Joe Johnson was making much of an effort, Darren thought eventually. And Craig didn't seem full of his usual tricks, either.

Maybe he'd got Craig sorted at last, thought Darren, hustling his friend as Craig took a pass from Joe Johnson and stopped it dead with his right foot. Then everything seemed to go into slow motion. Craig feinted to his left, nutmegged a totally bemused Darren . . . and went round him, laughing.

Darren turned, and was just in time to see Craig hammer the ball into the mini-goal. Behind it was the gaffer, who smiled at Craig, then looked at Darren, raised his eyebrows and wrote something down on his clipboard.

'Had you fooled there,' said a grinning Craig, punching Darren on the arm. 'I *love* this game,' Craig added. 'Born to boogie, born to score,' he sang like the crowd at the City stadium, 'watch him as he scores one more . . .'

Darren didn't say a word. He just wished Craig would vanish.

ELEVEN

By the time they were ten minutes into the practice game at the end of the session, Craig was beginning to think he'd never been happier in his life, even though the thickening drizzle had soaked him to the skin. His striking partner in the yellow-bibbed team was Joe Johnson – *Joe Johnson, of City FC!* – and he, Craig Hurst, had scored two peachy goals, one a nicely placed header from a free kick, the other a wicked, side-footed tap-in from a low cross.

Things don't get much better than this, he thought. And then they did.

A red team attack broke down on the edge of the yellow team's box, and Kevin – the yellows' big, fair-haired central defender – tidied up the ball, then pushed it on to that stocky, dark-haired midfielder. Craig knew now that the latter was called Ben Starkey, and also that he was a terrific playmaker, with more natural passing ability than Craig had ever seen in a player of their age.

Craig quickly glanced upfield, and saw that tonight's red team back four – Paul, Darren, Drew and a real hard-looking kid called Lee Powell at left full-back – were perfectly positioned across the pitch. They had two midfield players in front of them as well, Aaron and Curtis, both uncompromising tacklers. Joe Johnson was moving just ahead of Craig and to his left, and Jamie – also playing for the yellows – was steaming up on Craig's right.

Ben lofted a beautiful long ball to Joe Johnson, who took it on his chest, let it fall to his feet, then headed straight for Paul. Craig made a run towards the reds' box, bisecting the positions of Jason and Curtis, keeping the goal in his sights, expecting Joe Johnson to go for the byline and put over a cross. And that's exactly what he did, slipping past Paul and curling a high, teasing ball into the penalty area. But Darren called, *'Mine!'* then leapt to head it away.

It wasn't a great clearance. The ball looped high into the dark sky, but Darren hadn't got any distance on it. Craig could see it dropping in the glare of the floodlights, and judged it would come down just beyond the edge of the area, and to his right. From the corner of an eye he glimpsed somebody racing in beside him, and realized it was Jamie, and that Drew was already stepping up to block whatever Jamie might be intending to do if he got the ball.

'*Leave it!*' Craig yelled at the top of his voice, still running, gaze fixed on the slowly spinning, descending ball, his concentration total, freezing out every possible distraction of sound or vision. He instinctively adjusted his stride, then launched himself into the air – everybody watching thought he seemed to hang there for an age, his body parallel to the ground – and swung his boot to the spot where it would meet the ball on its downward trajectory.

The instant he made contact Craig knew the shot would be an absolute screamer. His instep hit the ball with maximum power, blasting it into the net, a white blur the keeper – a quiet kid called Sam – could barely have seen before it was far too late. Craig fell to the ground, his follow-through making him roll, but he was soon back on his feet again, his arms raised in triumph. He could hear applause and yells of appreciation coming from the touchline.

'Jesus Christ,' said Joe Johnson, running up, a look of real admiration on his face. Beyond him Craig could see Darren standing on the edge of the D, hands on hips, head down, and Sam retrieving the ball from the back of the net. 'That's got to be the best volley I've seen since the Garcia goal in the last World Cup,' said Joe Johnson. 'You got any Argentine blood in you?'

'Not that I know of,' Craig replied, grinning at him.

Craig looked towards the spectators. His father was standing on the touchline, sheltering from the rain under the big green golfing umbrella he had started to keep in the Frontera. Dad was giving him the thumbs-up, and Craig waved in acknowledgement, his deep pleasure in the goal he'd just scored only increasing as most of his team-mates came over to congratulate him. The gaffer's nod and smile seemed to say he was pretty pleased with him too.

The game finished twenty minutes later – yellows winning by a cool five goals to two, Ben and Joe Johnson scoring the fourth and fifth – and after the warm-down, Craig headed for the pavilion with the rest of the lads.

'Hang on, Craig,' called out Joe Johnson, and jogged over. 'You've forgotten something,' he added, tossing Craig the muddy ball. 'Score a hat trick, keep the ball. That's what happens when you're a pro, anyway.'

'He's not a pro yet,' said the gaffer, appearing

from behind Craig, 'and the board will have *my* guts for garters if we start giving a ball to every boy who scores three goals at training. I'm afraid the club's not that rich, Craig.'

'That's OK, gaffer,' said Craig, handing him back the ball. 'I don't mind.'

'Well, you should, son,' said another voice, loudly. Craig turned and saw three people coming towards them, his dad, Wayne Flynn's dad – the loud voice belonged to him – and Wayne himself, hurrying in tow. Craig's dad still had his big umbrella up, and Mr Flynn had a larger, blue one emblazoned with a Rovers crest. Mr Flynn was thickset and balding, and was wearing a green Rovers jacket. 'It wouldn't hurt this club to be less stingy,' he continued. 'Rovers are a lot more free with their money, I can tell you.'

'They can afford to be,' said the gaffer calmly, like a teacher dealing with a difficult parent, Craig thought – and that's just what Mr Flynn was, he suddenly realized. There had been plenty of talk among the lads and dads about the Davy Flynn inquiry. Wayne and his father had brazened it out, saying it was all just sour grapes and Davy's former club trying to make trouble for him. 'Did you want something, Mr Flynn?' the gaffer asked.

'Actually, I did,' said Mr Flynn aggressively. 'I wanted to tell you I don't like the way you've been playing our Wayne upfront; he's midfield, he's got a good engine on him, he's box to box all day long, right? And when are you going to settle on your first team? You've got this cup game coming, and if I were you, I'd aim at building your whole formation round Wayne...'

'If you *were* me, Mr Flynn,' said the gaffer, smiling, but with a steely edge to his voice, his eyes narrowed, 'you'd know I make a point of never discussing individual boys with their parents in public, or team selection – at any time. Now, if that was all, then I think we ought to let these young men get out of the rain and off home to their beds. Good night, Mr Flynn.'

Wayne's dad looked as if he wanted to continue the conversation, but the gaffer didn't give him the chance. He made for the pavilion, with Joe Johnson – who, Craig noticed, had been giving Mr Flynn a what-stone-did-*you*-crawl-out-from-under? stare – following. Craig nodded at his dad and went in the same direction, Wayne tagging along behind him. Wayne's father didn't move, his expression suddenly bad-tempered, his eyes on the gaffer.

'Is your dad always like that?' Craig asked as they went inside.

'Like what?' said Wayne. 'He was only trying to be helpful.'

'Oh yeah?' said Craig, turning to look at Wayne as they passed the gym. 'It sounded more to me like he was trying to tell the gaffer how to do his job. And if he thinks Rovers are so wonderful, why are you here, at City?'

'Because it just happens to suit us at the moment,' said Wayne haughtily, although Craig could see some uncertainty in him, too. 'I'll be moving on soon,' Wayne added. 'Dad's got something much better lined up for me.'

'What, exactly?' asked Craig, smirking. 'A girls' netball team? I wouldn't count on a first-team place, though. You're probably useless at everything.'

They had reached the doorway of the changing room itself. Wayne pushed in past Craig, then turned to face him. The room was full, steam from the shower room next door making it hazy and damp. Several of the lads near the door were sniggering, obviously having overheard some of the last exchange. But suddenly a tense, expectant hush fell, and everybody seemed to be listening, wondering if the confrontation might go further, maybe even lead to something tasty. Craig could see Darren looking at him and Wayne.

'You think you're *so* naffing good, don't you?' Wayne sneered, jabbing his finger at Craig like a weapon, but not actually touching him. Craig didn't react, although he didn't give any ground, either. 'Well, you know nothing about the way this game works, pal,' he went on. 'And you're going to find out there's a lot more to it than sticking the ball in the net. Much more.'

Wayne stomped off to his peg, the hush soon filling with banter again.

Craig stood there smiling for a second, just to show everybody in the room that he wasn't rattled. Then he shrugged and got changed quickly. He nodded goodbye to Darren and walked out to the car park, where engines growled and headlights cut through the cold, drizzly gloom as cars queued up to leave.

Craig's dad was waiting, and chattered cheerfully about the session all the way home. Craig was tired, but the memory of his goals kept him happy . . .

Although for some reason Wayne's words kept coming back to haunt him.

TWELVE

Darren stood between his dad and grandad on the touchline of the near pitch at Hawks' Nest, watching the first friendly of the season. It was a beautiful, crisp, late October morning, the sounds of boot on ball and players shouting sharp in the clear air, the sun shining in a washed-blue sky, a slight, fresh breeze chasing a few yellowed leaves across the short, dew-soaked grass.

But Darren was deeply fed up, as miserable as he could possibly be.

He sighed, hunched his shoulders, thrust his clenched fists even deeper into the pockets of his new tracksuit bottoms, a very early Christmas present from his gran and grandad. Darren absolutely loathed being a sub. He felt totally useless, and followed the action on the pitch hungrily with his eyes, his boots twitching, his legs shaking with a physical need to get out there and play.

'Come on, United!' bellowed a red-faced man further up the line. He was, presumably, the father of a Darbridge United player, Darbridge being City's opponents today, and he hadn't stopped yelling since the kick-off. Darren thought it was only a question of time before the gaffer told him to be quiet. 'For heaven's sake, pull your fingers out!' the man roared. 'Get stuck *in*!'

'Blimey, that bloke's really got a voice on him, hasn't he?' Grandad muttered. Darren's dad smiled, as did some of the other City dads nearby. 'Mind you, we can always hope he has a heart attack,' Grandad added. 'And he will if he keeps that up. How much longer is there to go, anyway, Darren?'

'About a minute less than the last time you asked, Grandad,' said Darren.

'Sorry, Darren,' said Grandad. 'I just want to see you playing out there. I don't think it's fair. Surely they'll put you on for a while, at least . . .'

Darren stayed silent. He desperately hoped his grandad was right, but with every second that ticked by it seemed less likely he would get onto the pitch this morning. And if he didn't . . . well, then he'd know his performance that Thursday night – when Craig had nut-megged him, and hit that incredible volley off his pathetic clearance – had probably finished his City career.

Darren didn't really think he'd done any better during the sessions on the following Tuesday or Thursday evenings, although nothing quite so disastrous had happened again, mostly because he had simply avoided getting into any one-on-one situations with Craig. He had also made sure in the practice games that he kept all his clear-ances as far away from Craig as possible.

But Darren knew he wasn't fooling the gaffer. Mr Shepherd had given him a talking-to after the nutmegging and the volley, the problem being, the gaffer had said, that Darren had panicked when he should have concentrated and stayed alert. From then on Darren had been aware of the gaffer watching him, that steady, unrelenting gaze noting every missed tackle and mistake.

Darren soon realized the tiny amount of confi-dence he'd started with was fast disappearing, that his entire game was going to pieces. By the end of the last session he'd become convinced he was definitely on his way out. But the gaffer hadn't taken him to one side and given him the bad news. Instead, he had gathered the lads around him and told them about Saturday's game.

At the time it had seemed to Darren like a reprieve, a chance – if only he could pull himself together – to show the gaffer what he could do. Darbridge United was a second division club, and Darren reasoned its youth squad team probably wasn't much cop. The game would be a friendly, too, sixty minutes divided into two halves of thirty minutes each, with plenty of substitutions.

Darren had therefore arrived at Hawks' Nest early that morning with high hopes. He had even started to feel excited when he'd gone into the changing room and seen the numbered red-and-black strip laid out for every boy in the squad, just as it would be for the first team squad in a Premiership game. The gaffer had said it was important they should all feel like professionals.

And that's how Darren *had* felt as he'd got changed and run out into the sunshine. But the good feeling had begun to fade when he'd discovered he wouldn't be playing in the opening period, especially with Wayne muttering that the eleven City lads on the pitch at the kick-off were bound to be the gaffer's preferred first team. Darren hadn't thought of that, but decided Wayne was probably right. And now the second period was almost over.

'Wakey, wakey, son,' said his dad suddenly. 'I think you're wanted.'

Darren glanced up the touchline and saw the gaffer gesturing for him to come over. Darren instantly pulled his hands out of his pockets and started jogging away from the watching men, his heart pounding wildly in his chest.

'Go for it, Darren!' he heard his grandad yell behind him, but Darren didn't respond, keeping his eyes fixed firmly on the group of people surrounding the gaffer. Des and Andy were there, as were the other City lads not playing at the moment – those who'd been on already, and the three or four like Darren who hadn't, among them a very unhappy, sulky-looking Wayne Flynn.

'Time to make a few changes, I think,' said the gaffer. 'Jamie, you're on for Kevin – I want to see you taking the ball to them, keep them worried, get some good crosses in. Wayne, you're on for Craig, and I want to see you keeping it simple, right? And Darren, you're on for Drew. OK, lads?'

'Yeah, boss,' they murmured in unison,

although Darren noticed Wayne managed to make the two words sound pretty surly. They stripped off their tracksuits, then did their warm-up routine as they waited for a stoppage which would allow them onto the pitch. The ref blew at last for a foul, Des called off the players who were being replaced, and the three substitutes ran on.

'Oh, and Darren . . .' the gaffer shouted. Darren stopped and looked round at him. 'See if you can't get a bit more organization into our defence. We're looking shaky, especially when they come at us. And relax, son. Got that?'

Darren nodded, then turned and trotted towards the City area, meeting a smiling Craig leaving the field with Kevin and Drew. Craig had every reason to smile, thought Darren. City were 2–0 in the lead, and Craig had scored both goals, generally making the Darbridge defence look pretty hopeless.

'I've softened them up nicely, Daz,' said Craig, smiling and raising his hands for a high-five. 'They definitely won't be any trouble for you now.'

'Naff off, Twink,' laughed Drew. 'It was me and Lee Powell that did the softening up, and you know it. All you strikers do is ponce around trying to look good. If you ask me, this lot might still have something in the tank . . .'

Darren soon found out Drew was right, Darbridge weren't a walkover. They brought on a couple of subs as well. One was fair-haired and smallish, but he was a busy, bustling ball-winner who immediately made a real impact in midfield, making life more difficult for Ben. The other was a tall, rangy striker, all elbows and knees, very physical in the box, good in the air.

And with Craig off the field, the United defence seemed to shake itself out of its collective torpor and start playing properly. Suddenly it was tougher for City, with Darbridge getting loads of possession and pressing very hard. Towards the end of the game they were on level-pegging – neither of the Darbridge goals Darren's fault, thank heavens – and City only just scraped a win, with Jamie scrambling a goal from a corner in the dying seconds.

The gaffer wasn't pleased, and told them in the changing room afterwards what they'd be doing in training during the next week to put things right. Darren wasn't happy, either. He hadn't played badly, but he hadn't relaxed, spending most of his time making panicky tackles and trying to get his fellow defenders organized. And he certainly hadn't shone, not like Craig.

But nobody was undermining Craig's confidence in himself as a player, Darren brooded as he got changed. Not like Craig was continually doing to him. And there wasn't a thing he could do about it, Darren thought . . .

Then something happened during the journey home from Hawks' Nest after the match, a small, chance event Darren could never have anticipated.

Craig's dad drove his car very fast, and the Frontera would usually be long gone by the time Darren's dad got them to the main road in the old van he used for work. But on this Saturday, Darren and his father had come in Grandad's Focus. Grandad drove pretty fast too, and they somehow stayed right behind the Frontera well into the suburbs, despite the Saturday traffic.

'Seems like your friend is getting a hamburger for his lunch,' said Darren's dad as the Frontera pulled into the car park of a roadside Burger Shack. Dad turned back to look at the traffic ahead, and Grandad didn't look round at all.

Darren craned round to peer out of the rear window . . . only to catch a brief glimpse of Craig and his father getting out of the Frontera, and a man walking towards them, a broad smile on his face, his hand outstretched in greeting.

A memory tugged at Darren, and suddenly he realized he'd seen the man before, on TV. It was John Vulpine, the agent involved with Davy Flynn.

THIRTEEN

Craig wasn't surprised when his dad suddenly pulled into the Burger Shack car park, although he was slightly puzzled when he said they were going to meet somebody there. He decided his dad must want to introduce him to a girlfriend. After all, Craig knew plenty of kids at school whose divorced parents were constantly moving in with new people or getting remarried.

So Craig was completely unprepared to find himself shaking hands with John Vulpine. Craig knew who he was before the agent introduced himself. Craig had only seen him once on TV, but the Flynn connection must have made the face stick in his mind, he thought. At any rate, nobody else in the busy car park seemed to be giving the man or his Jaguar a second look.

'Very pleased to meet you, Craig,' he said, releasing Craig's hand and smiling. John Vulpine

112

was tall and grey-haired and wearing brown brogues, beige casual slacks, and a green and yellow, diamond-patterned sweater, the sort Craig had seen golfers wearing on TV. 'I was very impressed by your scrapbook,' John Vulpine added. 'You're quite a prospect, young man.'

Craig had absolutely no idea what was going on, or how to respond. He looked to his dad for support, and some kind of explanation, but Dad didn't offer one, and the expression on his face wasn't giving anything away.

'Now you know why I wanted to hang on to it, Craig,' said Dad. 'And there's you probably thinking I was just a slow reader, right? Anyway, you must be starving after all that running about you've been doing – besides, I think we ought to get under cover. Those clouds are looking a bit ominous.'

A heaped mass of dark cloud was starting to fill the sky, and the breeze was turning into a cold wind. Dad led the way across the car park, his arm round Craig's shoulders, John Vulpine on Craig's other side. They went through the restaurant's glass doors, John Vulpine first, Craig and his dad following, Craig noticing that his father glanced behind them, then seemed to quickly scan the crowd of people inside. Craig suddenly felt very uneasy.

There were long queues at the counter, mostly families with kids, or teenagers showing off to each other. But it was a big Burger Shack, and it didn't take Dad long to find them a table. It was in a corner upstairs, near a window with a view onto the car park. Craig and John Vulpine sat facing each other while Dad went back downstairs to get their food and drinks.

'So, Craig, how did your game go this morning?' John Vulpine asked at last. 'It was against Darbridge, wasn't it? They've got a pretty good youth squad for a second division club . . . How many goals did you score, then?'

'Er . . . we won three–two,' Craig replied nervously, wondering how John Vulpine knew the game had been against Darbridge, then realizing his dad must have told him. 'I scored twice,' he said, and John Vulpine nodded slightly, almost as if that was exactly what he'd been expecting Craig to say.

Then John Vulpine started asking questions. Craig felt awkward sitting there talking to him. It wasn't the questions that made Craig uneasy – they were about football, and showed that John Vulpine understood the game, and had paid very close attention to Craig's scrapbook – it was more that Craig knew he shouldn't be talking to an agent at all. Especially not in public.

Craig hadn't really followed the news stories about the Davy Flynn inquiry – there wasn't much need, what with Wayne broadcasting his opinion on the matter at every training session – but one thing Craig did know was that clubs didn't like agents talking to boys who were already signed to youth squads. He was pretty sure there was even something about it in his City agreement.

So if the gaffer, or anybody from the club, found out he'd been talking to an agent, to John Vulpine of all people . . . well, Craig felt sick at the thought of what that might mean to his career at City. He wondered why his dad had arranged this meeting, and desperately willed him to hurry upstairs again.

'Here we are,' said Dad, returning at last, and sliding a heaped tray onto the plastic table. 'Chunky Burgers and fries for us, Craig, and Chili-Chicken Chunkettes for you, John. OK,' he added, setting out coffees for himself and John Vulpine, Coke for Craig, 'we can chat and eat at the same time, right?'

Craig didn't say anything, but kept his head down, slowly unwrapped his Chunky Burger, bit into it. The three of them ate in silence for a while, Craig on one side of the table, the two adults on the other, looking at him.

'I don't think Craig's feeling chatty at the moment,' the agent murmured. Craig thought the man's teeth seemed too white and too large for his mouth. 'Jimmy Shepherd's obviously been telling him horror stories about us wicked, predatory agents and the terrible things we get up to.'

'Craig's too savvy to fall for a load of tosh like that,' said Dad, reaching across the table to pat Craig's arm and winking at him. 'And he can make his own mind up, can't you, son? Although I'm sure that once he's heard what we have to say, John, he'll agree that he ought to move to a different club.'

Craig paused with his mouth open, then lowered his Chunky Burger. 'But why?' he said, glancing from his father to John Vulpine. 'I like City. I've *always* liked City, and the gaffer says I'm doing pretty good so far . . .'

'You could be doing even better somewhere else,' said Dad eagerly. 'Look, son, I don't claim to be a football expert, but even I can tell you're special. Ron Flynn said the same the first night I got talking to him. He also told me he didn't think City FC was a big enough club for you. And he should know.'

'They're in the Premiership, aren't they?' Craig said quietly, frowning.

'For how much longer, though?' asked John Vulpine. 'This is their third season in the top flight, they haven't been out of the bottom half once, and they spent most of last season in the drop zone. Believe me, Craig, they're a yo-yo club. A few seasons up, then back down again, and no trophies. Ever.'

'It all comes down to cash, Craig,' said Dad. 'The bigger clubs have more money, so they can provide better coaching and facilities. I know you think this Jimmy What's-His-Name is the bee's knees, but Ron's not impressed. Ron drove me over to the Rovers training ground the other day too, and you wouldn't credit the stuff they've got there. The whole place is incredible . . .'

Craig sat silently while his dad went into raptures about Rovers and what the club could do for his career. He felt upset by what Dad and John Vulpine had said about City, though he knew they had a point. City weren't as big a club as the Manchester Uniteds and Arsenals and Rovers of this world. But they were still Craig's favourite team, always had been, always would be. And going to Rovers – City's local rivals – would seem like a betrayal.

Yet Craig couldn't bring himself to speak up and say that he wanted to stay at City FC. He had never seen his dad so enthusiastic, had never heard him saying proper dad stuff like 'It's in your best interests, Craig,' or 'I'm only thinking of you, son.' Craig's mind was a whirl of confusion. If he argued with Dad, would it wreck things with him? And what if his dad was right?

'Hold on a second, Steve,' said John Vulpine, interrupting Dad's flow. 'I can see Craig's finding this difficult. I mean, we're running down his club, and he doesn't even think he should be speaking to me.' Craig glanced up at him. 'There's no need to worry, Craig,' he continued. 'I haven't approached you – your father came to me. So no rules have been broken.'

'And that's the way it was, Craig,' Dad added. 'Cross my heart. I'm new to football, wanted to find out a bit about the business side, look after your interests. So Ron gave me John's number and I called him for advice. And John said he thought it wouldn't do any harm if we looked further afield than City . . . Have you had enough to eat, son, or do you want some ice cream?'

Craig had Chunky Chocolate Chip, and sat eating it while his dad and John Vulpine talked, Dad saying that – for obvious reasons – scouts from other clubs couldn't come to watch Craig at the City training sessions or games. So how could they see him play? John Vulpine smiled mysteriously, tapped the side of his nose and told them not to worry, he would sort something out.

A few moments later they were shaking hands again and saying goodbye at the Burger Shack's entrance, then dashing through the car park in the pelting rain to their cars. Craig and his dad jumped into the Frontera, and soon they were back on the road, the wipers sweeping water from the windscreen, Dad cutting through the busy Saturday traffic.

'Are you sure about this, Dad?' said Craig. 'I mean, it all sounds a bit . . .'

'Relax, son,' said Dad, smiling at him. 'Nothing ventured, nothing gained, as they say, and besides, there's no harm done if it doesn't work out. Just trust your old dad to take care of things. Mind you, I wouldn't mention this to your mum . . . I think we should keep this a secret between us boys, right?'

Craig nodded, but he didn't feel happy. He didn't feel happy at all . . .

FOURTEEN

The image of Craig shaking hands with John Vulpine in the Burger Shack car park kept coming back to Darren that Saturday afternoon and evening. It was the first thing he thought of when he woke up on Sunday morning, and brooding about it at school on Monday instead of listening in his lessons nearly got him into trouble several times, which had been a bit awkward.

But Darren was too interested in working out the implications of what he'd seen to worry much about being told off. On Monday night he sat watching TV, his dad on the sofa next to him, Ashleigh and Gemma lying stretched out on the floor. Darren thought Craig and his dad had obviously arranged to meet John Vulpine at Burger Shack. And John Vulpine was the agent involved in Davy Flynn's transfer from his previous club to Rovers.

So maybe John Vulpine was going to help Craig change clubs as well.

It seemed like the simplest explanation – and the best possible one from Darren's point of view. Darren knew his friend wasn't supposed to talk to an agent, that it was against the rules, that the gaffer wouldn't be very happy if he found out. But what mattered to Darren was the idea of Craig leaving City, of Craig not being there to undermine his confidence any more.

Darren could sense a faint stirring of hope deep inside him. Things were still as tough as ever for his mum and dad – Mum was doing overtime this evening, and there had been more talk of major lay-offs at Dad's work – but if only he could get some of his confidence back, Darren thought, if only he could start playing as well as he knew he could, then it might all be OK.

Darren wished he could just ask Craig what was going on, but they went to different schools, and lived too far apart for Darren to simply drop in on him. They had exchanged mobile numbers, and Darren was half tempted to call or text him . . . but he finally decided not to. What would he say? And what chance was there that Craig would actually give him a straight answer?

No, he'd have to wait until the next training session, Darren thought, and try to get the truth out of Craig somehow. And there was always Wayne, Darren realized, sitting forward on the sofa. It was obvious the Flynns were the link between Craig and John Vulpine. There was no way Motormouth would be able to keep his trap shut, especially about something this big.

'You all right, Darren?' said his dad, breaking into Darren's thoughts. 'You're very quiet again this evening. In fact, you've been very quiet since you started at City, and your mum and I have been wondering whether . . .'

'I'm fine, Dad,' said Darren, and stood up, suddenly thinking that the sooner tomorrow evening arrived, the better. 'Is it OK if I go to bed now?'

'But it's only half past eight,' said Dad, surprised. Ashleigh and Gemma glanced round, obviously worried that if Darren went to bed, they'd have to go too. Dad had been letting them all stay up later on the evenings Mum worked and Gran and Grandad couldn't come, so he'd have a bit of company. 'You're not sickening for something, are you?' he said, looking concerned.

'Honestly, Dad, I'm fine, really,' said Darren, stepping over his sisters' legs and heading towards the front-room door. 'It's just, er . . . the gaffer says we need plenty of sleep when we're training. See you in the morning, OK?'

But Darren didn't sleep well that night, his mind far too full of questions, brooding about Craig and the Flynns and John Vulpine. The next day at school felt as if it would last for ever, and even the journey in Grandad's car from home to Hawks' Nest seemed to take much longer than usual. By the time they stopped and parked, Darren was almost bursting with impatience.

He jumped out of the car and ran through the car park, not looking back at his dad and grandad. It was dark, although for once it wasn't raining, and it wasn't that cold, either. Most of the lads were already changed and waiting on the floodlit near pitch, laughing and kicking a ball around. Darren dashed into the changing room, quickly got into his kit, dashed back outside again.

He scanned the groups of boys on the pitch, looking for Craig and Wayne. He couldn't see them at first, catching sight of them at last with their dads near one of the goals, the two adults ignoring them and talking to each other.

Beyond them on the far pitch the under-19s were standing in a semi-circle, listening to one of the coaches explain something with plenty of gestures.

'Hey, on your head, Dazza!' somebody suddenly shouted behind him.

Darren turned to where the voice had come from, and saw Drew more than twenty metres away, shaping to pass him the ball. Drew was usually pretty accurate over distance, so Darren was surprised when the ball sailed over him and bounced towards Wayne, Craig and their fathers. Darren chased after it, noticing that Wayne and Mr Flynn were deep in conversation now.

'Thought you needed the exercise!' yelled Drew, and laughed.

Darren gave him the old two fingers, and got the ball under control just before it trickled into the goal, where he was almost close enough to hear what Wayne and his dad were saying. But the conversation seemed to end abruptly, Wayne stomping off past the goal, making for the centre of the pitch and the biggest group of waiting lads. His face was flushed and angry.

Mr Flynn watched him go, face impassive, hands in his pockets.

'What's up with Motormouth?' Darren asked Craig, who had walked over to him, leaving his dad behind in a pool of darkness. 'Lost his rattle, has he?'

'How should I know?' Craig replied, his sharp tone making Darren look at him. But Craig didn't meet his gaze. 'Come on, the gaffer's out,' he continued.

Darren hurried after his friend, dribbling the ball to where the gaffer had gathered the other lads around him, and soon the warm-up began. Darren and Craig stuck together as usual, but Darren soon realized Craig wasn't his normal self. He was quiet, wrapped in his thoughts, obviously worried, Darren instantly recognizing the symptoms of anxiety he knew so well.

Wayne wasn't his normal arrogant, bumptious self, either. To Darren's amazement, he was completely silent during the warm-up, and stayed that way when they all paired off for skills work. He didn't do any show-boating – the term the gaffer used to describe the kind of greedy showing off with the ball that was Wayne's usual style – and seemed barely interested in what he was supposed to be doing, his face a sullen mask of unhappiness.

He didn't even smile when the gaffer told

them to line up for shooting practice. But everybody loved shooting practice, thought Darren, because it was always fun to hammer the ball and pretend you were your favourite star player scoring in a big match. And for Wayne and the other show-offs in the squad it was the perfect opportunity to strut their stuff in front of everybody.

As ever, the lads formed a queue on the edge of the box, Des or Andy laying a ball off to each boy running in, the gaffer commenting on the result. 'Laces, Jamie,' the gaffer said after Sam held Jamie's softly hit effort. 'Hit it through your laces, son, then you'll get more power. Your ball, Wayne . . .'

Wayne started an angled run so he could shoot with his left foot, Des tapping a ball across his path. Darren was standing at the rear of the queue with Craig, and quickly stepped sideways so he could see Wayne better. He was startled by the look of fury on his face. Wayne struck the ball with savage power, smashing it past a diving Sam. Somebody called out, 'Nice one, Motormouth!' but Wayne turned away, ignoring the praise.

'Whoa, did you see that?' said Darren, returning to his place in the queue.

'What?' said Craig absently, peering ahead. 'No, I'm sorry, I didn't.'

'Listen, Craig, are you OK?' whispered Darren, turning to look at his friend. 'I mean, you don't seem too happy . . .' Darren ground to a halt, searching for the words that would get Craig to tell him what was going on, sure he wouldn't want to give up his secrets easily. But Darren was wrong.

'Actually, I've got a bit of a problem . . .' Craig whispered straight back, glancing round, obviously checking that nobody else was close enough to hear what he was going to say. Then, and at quiet moments during training, he told Darren all about the meeting with John Vulpine, and how his father wanted him to leave City FC and join another club, maybe even Rovers.

'So what are you going to do?' Darren asked Craig at last, keeping his voice level, careful not to give away his feelings. The two boys were standing together by the touchline, having a drink before the practice game got under way. Darren looked round, saw Craig's father standing with Mr Flynn near the pavilion now, the two men smoking cigarettes, talking and laughing.

'I don't know,' said Craig, miserably. 'But you

will keep this quiet, won't you, Daz? If the gaffer finds out, I might be looking for a new club anyway.'

'Yeah, of course, I will,' Darren replied. 'I won't breathe a word.'

But behind his back, Darren's fingers were well and truly crossed.

FIFTEEN

It was amazing how a single secret could make your life very complicated, Craig brooded as he closed the front door of the flat behind him and trudged downstairs to the street. It was ten o'clock on a dank Sunday morning, and the sky was steel-grey. But then this was a pretty big secret, he thought, and keeping secrets wasn't something he'd done a great deal of in the past.

Craig's dad was in the Frontera, talking on his mobile, the same phone he'd used to call Craig last Wednesday before Mum had come home. Dad had said John Vulpine had arranged for Craig to play in a game on Sunday, and that someone important would be there. Craig had felt briefly excited, but his heart had sunk when he'd realized he'd have to start lying to his mum now.

He knew that he couldn't possibly tell her anything about the game at all.

The first lie hadn't been too difficult, especially as Dad had told him what to say – that he wanted to take Craig out on Sunday and spend time with him when he wasn't playing football. Mum had reluctantly gone along with the idea, much to Craig's relief. Then she had started asking questions, and Craig had discovered that one lie invariably leads to another, and another . . .

Mum had insisted on knowing where Dad would be taking him, whether he would be buying him lunch, what time he would be bringing him home. Then there had been the kit problem – Craig had known he'd never get past Mum with a sports bag on Sunday, and had decided to smuggle extra kit and his spare boots to training on Thursday, stashing it in the Frontera afterwards.

It had all been very difficult, he thought, opening the passenger door of the Frontera and climbing in, and it wasn't over yet. He just hoped he could get himself cleaned up properly after the game . . . But it would all be worth it in the long run, Dad had said – and Mum would just have to like it or lump it, Craig suddenly thought, his feelings towards her hardening. It was his life, and his father was the best person to help him find his way at the moment.

At least that's what Craig kept telling himself.

'Listen, it's Sunday,' his dad was saying into his mobile, 'so there's nothing I can do today. OK, I'll call you tomorrow, and that's a promise.' Craig watched his dad end the call and put the phone in his pocket, then sit frowning for a second. Eventually he turned to Craig and smiled. 'Right, son,' he said, 'we'd better get a move on. John wants us there by eleven.'

Dad drove off quickly through the quiet Sunday morning streets, Craig half wondering what his phone conversation had been about, although he soon put it out of his mind. He felt a little more nervous than usual. He knew that he would be playing for a Sunday league side, and that the rest of the team would be older than him. But Dad hadn't been able to tell him any more.

They travelled in the opposite direction from Hawks' Nest, deeper into the city, through areas Craig didn't know. They crossed the river, and finally reached a vast open space, a muddy green plain divided into what seemed like an infinity of football pitches, the roads nearby lined with parked cars. Everywhere Craig looked there were men and boys playing football.

Craig was relieved his dad seemed to know where to go, and soon they were turning off the road into a small car park with a rough cinder surface. Directly before them stood a long wooden shed, its sides and tar-paper roof blackened with age. Dad parked in the only space left, next to a Jaguar Craig recognized, and they got out, Craig with his kit in a Sainsbury's carrier bag.

John Vulpine was waiting for them by the doors into the shed. Wayne and Mr Flynn were there too, the latter in his Rovers coach jacket and a Rovers baseball cap. Mr Flynn was talking to another adult Craig didn't recognize, an older man wearing a waxed jacket and a flat cap. This man – who had a thin, sharp face and penetrating blue eyes – turned to look Craig up and down, openly giving him the once-over, making him feel very uncomfortable.

'Morning, Steve, Craig,' said John Vulpine, nodding at them. 'Glad you could make it. You know Ron and Wayne, of course, but let me introduce you to Bernie Walker . . .' The man shook hands with Craig's dad, and then with Craig. 'Bernie works as a scout for a, er . . .

132

certain well-known club, Craig,' John Vulpine explained, 'and he often comes here to check out the talent.'

'Yeah, and it's usually pretty thin on the ground,' said Bernie Walker, sighing. Then he turned his blue eyes back to Craig. 'So I'm hoping to see something a little better today. You come highly recommended, son.'

Craig didn't know what to say, and he was grateful when John Vulpine said they ought to get him into the shed to meet George, the manager of the team he'd be playing for, Walsey Spartans. The shed was divided into poky changing rooms, each smelling of sweat and liniment and urine, the floors littered with clumps of dried mud and cigarette ends, the showers ancient.

George, it turned out, was fiftyish and fat, and he was Mr Flynn's brother, which explained a lot, thought Craig, although he couldn't understand why Wayne had come to watch. But Craig didn't have time to worry about that. George took him into the Walsey changing room, Craig quailing a little when he saw that the team were mostly fifteen or sixteen, and pretty hard-looking, too.

'OK, lads, listen up,' said George, who was squeezed into a tracksuit too small for him, and wore expensive Nikes. 'Young Craig here will be playing upfront for us today, so just make sure he gets plenty of service early doors.' Nobody said anything, but Craig felt a dozen pairs of hostile eyes rake him from head to foot. 'And don't mess about. I want you all totally focused from the first minute, OK? Right, kick-off's in five minutes . . . have a good one.'

Somebody chucked Craig a damp, smelly green shirt with a number ten on the back. He got changed in silence, ignored by the others, slightly shocked to see a couple of them light cigarettes the instant George left the room, and to hear banter and mickey-taking laced with more inventive swearing than he was used to. Eventually everybody went outside, and Craig followed.

The sky was still grey, and a chill wind swept across the patchy, muddy, tussocky pitch. As he took up his position, Craig could see other games being played all around, hear the thump of boot on ball, players and supporters yelling. Walsey Spartans had won the toss and chosen ends, and their opponents – Craig couldn't be sure, but he thought he'd heard somebody say they were actually called Natural Born Killers FC – would be kicking off.

Craig glanced upfield and saw a defender

with a shaved head pointing at him and laughing. Another, bigger defender – the whole team seemed even older than the Walsey Spartans lot, and looked as if they'd just escaped from prison – stared coldly at Craig, slowly made a throat-cutting gesture, and grinned madly at him. Then the ref blew his whistle, and the game began.

It was a difficult match for Craig to get into. He had no idea what kind of formation his team was playing, or what their game plan was. Walsey had some decent players, but most of the opposition only seemed interested in seeing how much damage they could inflict on them in clattering tackles. Craig barely saw the ball in the first ten minutes, and was glad he hadn't.

Even so, he knew instinctively he was the best player on the park.

After a while he looked over at the touchline. His dad was there, hands in the pockets of his leather jacket, his face grim as he watched the game, the Flynns and John Vulpine and Bernie Walker there too, the scout looking bored and distinctly unimpressed. Craig thought he'd better do something.

Just then a Walsey defender put in a tackle and hoofed a huge clearance upfield. Craig carefully assessed the flight of the ball and the positions of the opposition players. Then he turned and made a run straight towards their box.

In front of him he saw the defender who'd made the throat-cutting gesture beginning to back-pedal, trying to keep Craig and the descending ball in sight at the same time. Craig sped on, the defender chasing and grabbing his shirt, but Craig shook him off, the ball coming down over Craig's shoulder and between them. Craig trapped it and stopped dead, the defender flying past.

'Why, you little—' he heard the defender hiss, but ignored him.

Craig looked up, saw the keeper was off his line, and – cool as you like – chipped him, the ball looping agonizingly over the astonished keeper's head and dropping sweetly into the goal. Craig turned round. He smiled and made a pistol shape with his right hand, his thumb cocked, his forefinger pointing at the defender he'd beaten – who was now staring at him open-mouthed.

'Pow,' said Craig, blew across his fingertip, and holstered his hand.

'Brilliant, son!' he heard his dad calling out. 'Absolutely brilliant.'

Craig looked at the touchline and saw his

dad and Mr Flynn grinning now, Bernie Walker
smiling and nodding at John Vulpine . . . and
Wayne staring.

Even from a distance Craig could see the hate
in Wayne's eyes.

SIXTEEN

On Tuesday evening Darren sat in the Hawks' Nest changing room after the session, trying to screw up the courage to go and speak to the gaffer. The lads had long since changed and gone, and Darren was there alone in the silence after their noise, his packed kitbag on the bench beside him. He told himself for the fiftieth time that grassing on Craig was the right thing to do.

Of course, he thought, poking at a clump of dried mud on the floor with the toe of his trainer, it was also definitely the wrong thing to do. The gaffer had rules, but rule one among the lads was simple – *Thou Shalt Not Grass on a Mate*, whatever the circumstances. It was a key part of a code Darren had always stuck to, a principle he was finding it hard to abandon.

He wouldn't have to do it if Craig left City, he thought. But what if Craig didn't leave? What if every training session was going to be the same, with Craig the perfect striker running rings round dozy Dazza, making him look a total dipstick? No, Craig had to be got rid of, Darren thought grimly, and the sooner the better. He grabbed his kitbag and marched off, determined.

Darren pushed open the changing-room door and went into the corridor beyond. The gaffer was coming out of his office, pulling on his coat, shutting his door behind him. The instant Darren saw him his determination vanished.

'You still here?' the gaffer said, smiling and striding down the corridor, switching off lights as he went. Darren fell in behind him, stumbling along, nearly tripping over his kitbag. 'I'm glad you are, though,' said the gaffer as they passed the gym and the physio suite. 'I meant to say, Roy Newton and I want to speak to you about something before training on Thursday, OK?'

They went outside, the gaffer stopping to lock the pavilion's main doors. Then he turned and looked at Darren, obviously waiting for him to respond.

'On Thursday,' Darren mumbled. 'You and – and . . . Mr Newton.'

'That's right,' said the gaffer. 'See you about quarter to seven?'

He headed towards his silver Volvo across the

dark car park, the sole illumination coming from a couple of security lights near the exit now the floodlights had been turned off. He nodded as he passed Darren's dad, who was standing by the van, the only other vehicle there. Darren followed, and soon he and his dad were leaving Hawks' Nest behind them in the gloom.

'You took your time getting changed tonight, didn't you?' said Darren's dad, glancing round at him. 'I nearly froze to death waiting for you out there. I'm just glad I'm not a brass monkey. Anyway, everything all right, son?'

Darren grunted a 'Yeah' at him, and his dad gave him a funny look. But Darren ignored it, and his dad didn't ask him anything else. When they got home, Darren refused his mum's offer of some toast and a drink of milk. He went straight upstairs and got ready for bed. He lay rigid under his duvet, staring at his Tony Adams poster, a single question burning in his mind.

What were the gaffer and Roy Newton going to say on Thursday?

It could only be one thing, he thought, recalling a cross he hadn't cleared during the practice match, a tackle he'd missed, picking at the memories like scabs. Darren was sure the gaffer had finally decided to kick him out of the City youth squad, the fact that Mr Newton would be there making it even more certain. Although maybe grassing on Craig could save him somehow . . .

Darren slept badly, unable to stop worrying, going over his fears in his mind again and again, trapped in a seemingly endless tape-loop of anxiety. At breakfast the next morning he was monosyllabic, almost silent. He brooded all day at school, and by teatime he felt as if he was about to explode.

And then he did. Everyone was there – Gran and Grandad, Mum and Dad, Ashleigh and Gemma – but it wasn't a particularly happy gathering. Gran and Grandad were a bit tetchy with each other, Mum and Dad were tired and grumpy, Ashleigh was cross about something, and Gemma was whiny.

'So, Darren,' said Grandad, smiling at him eventually, obviously trying to lighten the fractious mood around the table. 'How are you getting on with your football? I'll bet you're looking forward to training tomorrow.'

'Actually, I'm not,' said Darren, dropping his knife and fork on his plate with a clatter that made the others jump. 'And I'm not going,' he went on, his voice rising, his eyes prickling with tears. 'In fact, I'm not going to City again,' he shouted at them. 'I'm a *crap* football player, OK?'

Then he stood up, roughly pushed back his chair, and stormed out of the dining room, slamming the door behind him. He heard Grandad plaintively asking, 'What did I *say*?' but Darren stamped on, heading upstairs to his room. He flung himself face down on the bed and let the hot tears flow.

A few moments later he heard a soft knock-knock on his door, his mum asking quietly if he was all right. He ignored her. Then he heard the door opening, someone coming in and sitting down on the bed beside him. Mum softly squeezed his hand. He pulled it away from her, didn't turn round.

'Come on, Darren, talk to us,' his mum whispered, leaning across him. Darren could feel her warm breath on his ear, smell that Mum scent he could remember from when he was little and she used to cuddle him if he fell over and got hurt. 'We're worried about you,' she said. 'What's the matter, love?'

'We *thought* something was wrong,' said another voice, Darren realizing his dad must be in the room too. 'We could talk to Mr Shepherd if you like.'

'There's no point,' said Darren . . . and before he could stop himself he'd sat up and was telling his mum and dad how the gaffer and Mr

Newton wanted to see him before training on Thursday, and how he'd really tried at City so he could earn enough one day to pay all the bills, but he was sure he'd totally blown it, and he was sorry but he couldn't handle it any more, and then he was crying again and his mum and dad were both hugging him.

'Well, you've got yourself into a right old state, haven't you?' said Mum at last when he'd managed to calm down and they'd stopped hugging. She smiled and pulled a tissue from her sleeve, wiped his eyes, then handed it to him so he could blow his nose. Which he did, loudly. 'And whatever gave you this idea that *you* have to pay our bills?' Mum said, looking puzzled.

'I . . . I don't know,' said Darren, feeling uneasy now, avoiding her gaze. The answer was that he didn't think his parents could do it themselves, and he didn't want to admit that, even to himself. It lessened them, somehow.

'I bet I do,' said his dad, standing up suddenly. 'It was us, Jeanie. He's always been a terrible worrier, hasn't he? And this last few months we've done nothing but moan about money, and having too many bills to pay, and not enough overtime, and he's taken it all in. Then he gets into City and we all start talking about how he might turn out to be the next Davy Flynn . . .'

'And make a fortune, and solve our problems,' Mum said, turning to Darren and sounding guilty. 'We've said stuff like that a few times, haven't we? Oh, Darren, no wonder you've been looking as if you were carrying the whole world on your shoulders. We were only joking, honestly. Although I suppose we should have realized you might think we were serious . . .'

Darren looked at her and shrugged, not knowing what to say.

'We're the ones who should be sorry, Darren, not you,' said Dad firmly, sitting on the bed once more and putting his arm round him. 'Listen, I swear we're not expecting anything from you if you make it as a professional – and we never will do, either. You're a good boy to think about helping us, but it's our job to take care of *you*. Have you got that absolutely straight, son?'

'Yes, Dad,' Darren replied, examining his parents' faces, realizing they meant what they'd said, feeling his burden lift slightly. But not entirely. 'What about the bills, though?' he asked, anxiously. 'What happens if you get laid off, Dad, and we don't have enough money to pay them all? I mean, will we lose the house? And where will we live if we do? And what about . . . ?'

'Whoa there, slow down, love,' said his

mum. 'We've kept going this long, and we're not beaten yet. We'll sort something out, you'll see.'

'We most certainly will,' muttered Dad, almost to himself, thought Darren, noticing a determined expression pass quickly across his father's face.

'Anyway, you'd better come and make friends with your grandad,' said Mum. 'He thinks it was his fault. We'll forgive you the bad language,' she added, giving Darren her mock stern frown. 'But just this once, mind . . .'

'And don't worry about Thursday,' said Dad as the three of them went out of the bedroom. 'Believe me, son, from where I've been standing on the touchline I'd say you've been more than keeping your end up. Mr Shepherd and Mr Newton probably want to ask you how things are going, that's all.'

For a second Darren allowed himself to hope his dad might be right.

Then he decided he still wasn't looking forward to the next day.

SEVENTEEN

The Flynn residence was much smaller and a lot less flashy than Craig had expected, he thought as his dad slowed down and parked the Frontera in the street outside. The street itself was pretty ordinary, the house an old red-brick terrace job, its small front garden converted into a paved off-road parking space. But the two cars standing there – Mr Flynn's Cherokee, and a brand-new, metallic-green VW Golf cabriolet – were more than flash enough.

'John's here already,' said Craig's dad as they got out of the Frontera, nodding at a Jaguar nearby, familiar even in the late-afternoon gloom. They edged past the Cherokee and the Golf and came to a glassed-in porch. Dad pressed the doorbell button, and they heard the first notes of the old *Match of the Day* theme tune echoing inside the house. 'He must be keen to give us some good news,' Dad said, turning to Craig and smiling. 'You all right, son?'

'I'm fine, Dad,' said Craig, thinking how much better he was getting at telling lies. He wasn't all right, he was worried – worried about what John Vulpine might have to say, worried about what he should do, worried about getting home before his mum, who didn't know Dad had turned up out of the blue to collect him after school. But Dad wouldn't want to hear any of that.

The frosted glass inner-porch door opened, and suddenly there before them was Mr Flynn. He was wearing a light-green replica Rovers shirt that was stretched tight over his bulging stomach, brand new Adidas tracksuit bottoms, white tennis socks and leather carpet slippers. He pulled open the outer door.

'Come in,' he said, beaming at them, his round face red and shiny. They followed him into a narrow hallway, the stairs to the bedrooms blocked by a heap of shopping bags. 'Excuse the mess,' said Mr Flynn, 'but the wife's just been on a bit of a spending spree. Again. Between you and me, she could shop for England. Oh, there you are, love. Any chance of some tea?'

A woman had appeared in the kitchen door-way. She was small and thin and about the same age as Mr Flynn, with blond-streaked hair arranged in an intricate hairdo, a deep-orange sunbed tan, and was wearing a tight red top, light-blue jeans with a crease down each leg, and strappy high-heeled shoes. She glared at her husband, then turned and shut the kitchen door on them.

Mr Flynn didn't seem very bothered, though. He laughed and pulled a naughty-boy face, then ushered Craig and his dad into the small front room. At one end of the room was a net-curtained window looking out onto the street, and at the other, sliding glass doors leading to a tiny garden. The floor was covered by a pink and blue carpet with a flower pattern, most of it obscured by a leather three-piece suite and a colossal widescreen TV.

'Steve, Craig, great to see you both!' said John Vulpine, rising from the sofa to shake their hands. He was wearing a dark suit and had been sitting next to Wayne, who stayed where he was. Craig realized Wayne looked just like his mum. It was the laser-eyed glare that did it, Craig thought, turning away in disdain. 'That was some performance on Sunday, Craig,' John Vulpine was saying. 'Bernie Walker told me he was very impressed.'

'So was my brother,' said Mr Flynn. He sat in one of the armchairs, and motioned everybody else to sit down too. John Vulpine and Craig sat on the sofa, Craig's dad taking the other armchair. 'George told me to say you can play for him any time,' Mr Flynn went on. 'Nobody scores five goals in a single match in that league and lives to tell the tale. Not usually, anyway.'

That didn't surprise Craig. After his first goal, he'd needed all his skill to avoid being badly injured. Every time he had got the ball, the defender who'd made the throat-cutting gesture had simply tried to scythe him down, the referee not taking any notice. One tackle had left some nasty stud-marks high on Craig's thigh, the red weals surrounded by a purple bruise and still sore three days later. Craig had left a few stud marks of his own, though.

'A class striker can always take care of himself when he needs to,' said John Vulpine. 'And Bernie definitely thinks you're a class act, Craig. So Walsey Spartans are going to have to do without your services, I'm afraid.'

'I take it Rovers *are* interested, then,' said Craig's dad, eagerly.

'Ah, now I didn't say that,' said John Vulpine, smiling. 'Rovers are a highly responsible football club, and they're not in the business of poaching young prospects from another club's youth squad. I'm a highly responsible agent, too, and I wouldn't be involved in anything like that, would I, Ron?'

'No, John, you wouldn't,' said Mr Flynn, grinning at him. Craig could see his dad was looking from John Vulpine to Mr Flynn and back again. His dad seemed a little confused, his forehead creased by a frown. 'What's the word on the inquiry, anyway, John?' said Mr Flynn. 'I heard it's not going ahead.'

'You heard right,' said John Vulpine, getting a pack of cigarettes from a pocket, offering them to Craig's dad and Mr Flynn, then taking one himself. 'There was no case. Nobody can prove I spoke to Davy or you, or to Rovers about Davy, *before* he'd left his former club. No rules broken, end of story.'

'So let me get this straight,' said Craig's dad, smiling now and leaning across Craig to take a light from John Vulpine's gold Ronson. He inhaled, then let smoke flow from his nostrils. 'If Craig leaves City, we can do what we like, and no-one can complain. Not City, not the FA, nobody?'

'That's the way it is, Steve,' said John Vulpine, drawing on his cigarette. 'After all, nobody outside this house knows you're here. And nobody at City knows you've met me, or that Craig played for Walsey Spartans, or that I might have had anything to do with Bernie Walker coming to watch him . . .'

He was wrong, Craig thought, his stomach suddenly clenching anxiously at the memory of the conversation he'd had with Darren at Hawks' Nest. Darren knew all about John Vulpine, and that meant he could blow this whole thing wide open if he wanted to. But Darren wouldn't do that, Craig decided. There was no way he would ever grass on him. Darren was a mate.

'Well, I think this is definitely turning into a good day for us, Craig,' said his dad, 'a very good day indeed. It looks like we'll be having a final word with your Mr Shepherd, and then you can make tracks for pastures new, somewhere a lot more . . . *rewarding* than City. You OK with that, son?'

Craig knew this was the moment for him to say no, he definitely wasn't OK with any of that. But he looked into his dad's eyes, the eyes that were the same colour as his own, and he saw the eagerness in them, and he couldn't do it. Craig wasn't even sure if that was how he truly felt, part of him feeling guilty and miserable, part of him thrilled his father was doing this for him.

'Yeah, Dad,' he said at last, and tried to raise a smile. 'Why not?'

'Good boy,' said his dad, patting Craig's arm and looking over his head at John Vulpine. 'So we just need to be careful about our timing – right, John?'

'Absolutely, Steve,' said John Vulpine. 'There are a few other details we should iron out, none of which young Craig probably wants to listen to . . .'

'Wayne,' snapped Mr Flynn, frowning at his son, 'take Craig upstairs and show him your new computer, or something. I'll go and see about that tea . . .'

Wayne sulkily rose from the sofa and trudged out of the room. Craig followed him, picking his way through shopping bags as they climbed the stairs to a landing. They passed a closed door with a sign saying DAVY'S ROOM – LITTLE BROTHERS SHOT ON SIGHT, thumping, loud rap coming through it, Wayne finally banging open the next door along and entering his bedroom.

It was much the same size as Craig's, but shabbier, the walls almost completely covered in posters, each one showing a famous striker, the bed old and battered, the floor heaped with clothes. A lap-top sat on a desk under the window, a big TV set and video on a shelf unit beside it, a DVD player beneath them, DVDs below that, a games console at the bottom, all new.

'Nice computer,' said Craig. 'Are you sure you know how to use it?'

'Oh yeah, I am,' said Wayne. He was lying on his bed, feet crossed, hands behind his head, staring at Craig and smiling enigmatically. 'And I'm sure of something else, too. You've got no idea what's going on here, have you?'

'At least I know my dad's taking care of my career for me,' said Craig, lightly tapping the lap-top's keyboard. 'And your dad doesn't seem to have moved you on to something better yet. Or isn't that going to happen now?'

'Never you mind *my* dad,' said Wayne, sitting up, his smile vanishing, his eyes narrowing, his face turning mean and ugly with hatred. 'Your dad isn't so perfect, pal. You want to ask yourself what's in all this for him. I know you think the sun shines out of his backside. But it doesn't . . . and he's in real trouble, too. He's only interested in you because you're his way out of it.'

'What are you talking about?' said Craig quietly, suddenly going cold.

So Wayne told him, and Craig listened, and his whole world fell apart.

EIGHTEEN

That Thursday evening, Darren's grandad drove the Focus through the open gates at Hawks' Nest and stopped in the car park. It was very dark, and the floodlights over the pitches were on, illuminating a few lads already changed and kicking a ball around. Darren was in the back seat and reached for the door handle, but didn't get out. His dad and grandad turned to look at him.

'I still think you ought to let me come with you, son,' said his dad.

'Your dad's right,' said Grandad. 'You might need moral support.'

'No, it's OK,' Darren replied, opening the door and letting the cold, wet wind whip into the warm interior of the car. At dinner the previous evening, when Dad had suggested coming along to the meeting with Mr Shepherd and Mr

Newton tonight, Darren had said yes. But then he'd thought about it, and decided it was something he should face alone. 'I'll be fine, really,' he said.

'Well, if you're sure . . .' said his dad, his expression one of anxiety for him, Grandad's the same, Darren suddenly noticing how much they looked like each other, like father and son, even though they were grown men. Darren's dad sighed, then reached out and squeezed Darren's shoulder. 'Good luck, son,' he said. 'And don't forget, all that matters to us is that you're happy.'

'Thanks, Dad,' said Darren, grabbing his kit-bag and getting out. 'I won't.'

Dad and Grandad got out too, and Darren walked away, only glancing back once to see them both smiling and nodding and giving him the thumbs-up.

Darren trudged on, went inside the pavilion. He went past the empty gym and the physio suite, past the changing rooms, caught a brief glimpse of the lads through a half-open door, heard their banter and jokes and loud laughter, and wondered how much longer he was going to be part of it all.

The gaffer's office door was closed. Darren stood before it, convinced that beyond this point the future direction of his entire life would change. Panic stirred in him, bringing with it from the depths again the idea of grassing on Craig to save himself . . . but he forced it back down. No, he thought, he didn't want to be that kind of person, not in a million years, not at any price.

He raised his head, squared his shoulders, took a deep breath, knocked.

'Come in!' the gaffer called out, and Darren opened the door. The gaffer was sitting at his desk, and Mr Newton was leaning against the wall near the window, holding a mug. There was another mug on the desk, next to a blue folder that was open, the gaffer studying a form he must have taken from it, a picture pinned to the corner. Darren realized it was his application form, with a couple of new sheets added. 'Sit down then, Darren,' said the gaffer.

Darren did what he was told, perching on the edge of the plastic seat in front of the gaffer's desk, carefully placing his kitbag on the floor beside him. He could feel a pulse beating in his left temple, and his mouth was very dry. He glanced at Mr Newton, who nodded and smiled at him, then sipped from his mug. Finally the gaffer lowered the form and looked up.

'Well now, Darren,' he said, leaning forward, his forearms on the desk, linking his hands and slowly tapping his thumbs together. The gaffer smiled, glanced at Roy Newton, then back at Darren, who swallowed nervously. 'I've been keeping a close eye on you these last few weeks,' the gaffer continued, 'and I must say . . . I think you've made excellent progress.'

'I . . . I have?' said Darren, eyes wide, his voice squeaky with surprise.

'Yes, your stats are looking good,' said the gaffer, checking the papers in front of him once more. 'I know you've had a few problems with Craig, but he *is* exceptional, and your tackle average is still around eighty per cent, your interceptions are about the same, and your clearances are improving.'

'They are?' said Darren, trying to keep his voice steady. 'I thought . . .'

'But there's something else about you,' said the gaffer, 'something I liked from the moment I saw it. That first practice game, you were the one who stepped up, tried to make a tackle on Craig, took responsibility. You've done the same lots of times since . . . which is why I'd like you to fill a special role for us, son. I'd like you to be under-fourteen team captain. What do you say?'

Darren sat motionless and silent for a second, his mouth open, gazing at the gaffer. Then he closed his mouth and grinned happily at the two men.

'We'll take that as a yes then, shall we?' said Mr Newton, smiling at Mr Shepherd, who smiled too and leaned back in his chair. Mr Newton laughed. 'I haven't seen a lad looking so shocked since the day we told Joe Johnson Mike wanted him for the first team even though he was only sixteen,' he said. 'But from what Jimmy says, you definitely deserve it. Congratulations, son.'

'Yes, congratulations, Darren,' said the gaffer, both men taking turns to shake his hand. Darren still felt a little dazed and confused, hardly daring to believe this was really happening. But it was, he realized. It was . . . 'I'm sure you'll do a terrific job,' the gaffer was saying to him, 'starting with the match this Saturday, of course. You'd probably like a look at the team sheet . . .'

The gaffer got a sheet of paper out of a drawer and laid it on the desk for Darren to study. Darren looked at it, but the names swam before his eyes. He was finding it hard to concentrate. Great changes were going on inside him, the worry that had filled his whole being suddenly starting to drain away.

Darren thought about Saturday's match, and what it would mean to be the one making decisions on the pitch. If they won that game, and kept winning, they'd get to the final, and if they won that, well, there was simply no telling what might happen after. But being captain was a pretty big job, he thought, and he wondered if he was up to it, the worry starting to come back again . . .

Then Darren realized that yes, he was more than up to it, that this was something he'd been waiting his whole life to do, that he just needed to get a grip on himself. He'd been given a golden opportunity, and he wasn't going to blow it now. That would be letting himself down, leave alone anybody else.

'So, what do you think of your team then, skipper?' asked Mr Newton, breaking into Darren's thoughts. Darren looked up at him, then looked down again and focused on the neatly typed list. He was the first of the lads to see it, he thought, the special privilege in that making him feel as if he'd somehow taken a big step away from being a boy and towards being something else . . .

The lads in the squad had talked endlessly about who would be in the starting eleven for the cup game, everyone's good qualities and weak points being discussed in enormous detail, and Darren smiled when he saw how wrong most of them had been. Sam was in goal, Paul at right back, Lee on the left, Drew and Darren in the centre of defence, the 'C' in brackets next to his name making him feel as if his heart would almost burst with pride.

Jamie was down for the right side of midfield, Ben in the centre, Jason on the left, Curtis in the hole supporting the two strikers, who were Craig and Wayne, the only name that made Darren pause for a second. But then he saw the gaffer's logic, remembering the sheer power of Wayne's shooting at practice, and Wayne's preference for his left foot, Craig favouring his right. They had the potential to be a great striking partnership, Darren thought.

Although the fact that they seemed to hate each other might make playing so closely together rather difficult, Darren realized. In any case, Craig might be leaving the club, which meant they'd be losing their best player anyway. Now Darren desperately didn't want that to happen, but he couldn't grass on Craig and get the gaffer to sort it out. So he would just have to do it himself.

'I think it's a good balance,' he said, scanning

the names of the substitutes, finally looking up and glancing from Mr Newton to the gaffer.

'Well, we're in agreement there,' said the gaffer. 'But we'll still need our wits about us on Saturday, that's for sure. Warlington won't be a walkover.'

'Huh, not with old Tony Rosemount running their youth squad,' said Mr Newton. 'If I didn't know better I'd say he was almost as wily as you, Jim.'

'I'll take that as a compliment,' said the gaffer, laughing again. 'Right, Darren,' he said, standing up. 'Let's go and tell the rest of the lads your good news.'

Darren left the office with the gaffer and Mr Newton, only half listening to the latter saying something about Mike Wilmot coming to the game on Saturday with some directors and some people from QuickPhone, and how important this was, but not grasping why. Darren swiftly got changed, then hurried outside to join the gaffer and Mr Newton, who had gone on ahead.

They rounded up the lads and made the announcement, Darren smiling and blushing as everybody cheered and yelled, 'Dazza for Eng-land!' and shouted rude comments and generally gave him one of those moments he'd probably remember for ever. Everybody, that is, except Wayne and Craig. Wayne had an air of smugness about him, and Craig looked more miserable than ever.

The captain of the City under-14s could see he had plenty of work to do.

NINETEEN

It was a bitterly cold evening, a real foretaste of winter, but that wasn't the reason Craig felt strangely numb. Like most of the other lads, he'd kept his tracksuit on and wore a woollen hat and gloves even after they'd done their warm-up routine, his face the only part of him exposed to the sharp wind that was driving the stinging rain almost horizontally across the floodlit pitches.

The numbness was inside, and it filled him completely.

They were playing two-touch, in groups of six divided into teams of three, the idea being that each player was only allowed to touch the ball twice. So the second touch had to be a pass or a shot, a third meaning possession went to the other side. Craig usually enjoyed it, the exercise being good for the skills strikers needed. But tonight he was just going through the motions.

From time to time, fragments of the conversation he'd had with Wayne the night before bobbed up into his mind, bringing back the shock of hearing something laid bare, something Craig knew he should have realized a long time ago and hadn't. Then the fragments sank into the cold numbness inside him once more, and all that remained was the tap-tap of boot against ball.

After a while the gaffer told them to take a break, and Craig watched as the others went off to get a drink from the water bottles Des and Andy were handing out on the touchline. Craig stayed where he was, keeping the ball from the exercise between his feet, his back turned to the touchline on the car park side. Eventually he saw Darren leaving the others and coming over.

'You OK, Twink?' asked Darren, stopping in front of him.

'I'm fine,' Craig replied, tapping the ball from foot to foot.

'Yeah, sure, that's why you look as if you want to blow your brains out, mate,' said Darren, glancing towards the centre circle, where the gaffer stood chatting to Paddy McKee, the club's goalkeeping coach. 'Is it to do with you going to Rovers?' he asked, turning to Craig again and whispering. 'Have you been talking to that agent? You haven't signed anything, have you?'

'It's my dad who's been doing all the talking,' said Craig quietly, still tapping the ball, not looking Darren in the face. 'And nothing's settled.'

'Good, well, that's OK then,' said Darren, Craig hearing the relief in his friend's voice. 'I, er . . . know it's not my business,' Darren continued, 'but I honestly don't think you should leave, Craig, I think you should stay here at City, with the gaffer and your mates. It's going to be really great, you'll see.'

'Even with Motormouth as my striking partner?' said Craig, looking up and into Darren's eyes, just visible below the edge of his black woolly hat, the silver Hawks logo sitting squarely in the middle of his forehead.

'The gaffer obviously thinks you'll make a good pair,' said Darren. 'And so what if Wayne is a pain in the neck sometimes. He's not *that* bad, is he?'

Craig stopped tapping the ball and let it slowly roll away from him. The slight pleading edge in Darren's voice had penetrated his numbness, that and the sheer surprise of hearing Darren say Wayne Flynn wasn't 'that bad'.

Then Craig realized what was going on. He knew Darren was talking to him partly because they were mates. But Darren wasn't merely one of the squad any more, he was captain, and Craig could see he was already trying to do his best for the team. And Craig couldn't help admiring Darren for that.

'Jesus, Dazza,' Craig said at last, deciding not to let Darren know he'd worked out what he was up to. 'You've changed your tune, haven't you? I thought we were the founder members of the I Hate Wayne Flynn Club.'

'Yeah, well,' said Darren, embarrassed, but smiling. 'He's got a pretty wicked shot, he's sharp in the box . . . and I can lend you some earplugs.'

'I could have done with those last night,' Craig murmured, and Darren gave him a questioning look. Craig shrugged. 'We were round at Wayne's house, and he told me some things I didn't really want to hear,' he said.

That was one way of putting it, thought Craig, remembering the anger in Wayne's voice the evening before. Craig realized where it had come from, too, having forced Wayne to admit his dad wasn't moving him, and certainly not to Rovers, even though Mr Flynn didn't think much of City FC, or the gaffer. Which seemed to imply that Mr Flynn didn't think much of Wayne.

Craig had soon discovered that Wayne thought Davy was their father's favourite. It was easy to see why, with Mr Flynn insisting on Wayne playing midfield even though he wanted to be a striker – which was Davy's position. From what Wayne had said, it almost seemed as if Mr Flynn simply didn't want him to do as well as his older brother . . . Craig wondered how Mr Flynn would react to the gaffer playing Wayne upfront in Saturday's game.

Then Craig remembered what else Wayne had said, and felt numb again. He knew now that Wayne had been jealous, resenting the fact that no-one was trying to make Craig play in a position he hated, the way Craig talked about what his dad was doing for him, the stupidity Craig had demonstrated for the last few weeks. And that's what it had been, Craig thought, complete and utter stupidity. But Wayne had quickly put him straight, and no mistake.

'Listen, Craig,' said Darren, 'if there's anything I can do to help . . .'

'Thanks, Daz,' said Craig. 'But there isn't. Come on, we're wanted.'

He trotted off towards the centre circle, where

the gaffer was organizing the lads for the practice game. The starting eleven for Saturday played the others, working on tactics and set pieces, the gaffer getting them to go over things again and again until they got it right. But Craig knew he wasn't playing well, and for the first time in a practice game he didn't score.

Wayne banged in a couple, though, and the gaffer seemed satisfied enough with the way the team was shaping up. He gave them the usual brief rundown of what he thought they needed to improve on – the lads had decided to call the gaffer's regular little end-of-session homily 'the sermon' – and sent them in to get changed. Craig didn't hang around, and was out in a few minutes.

His dad was waiting for him in the Frontera, talking on his mobile.

'Right, John, I'll speak to you tomorrow,' he was saying as Craig took his place in the front passenger seat and put on his seat belt. 'OK, son?' his dad asked, slipping the phone into the pocket of his leather jacket. Craig didn't reply, and his dad drove off, wheels spinning, and soon they were whizzing along dark country roads, headlights spookily illuminating trees and hedges.

Craig's dad chattered about Craig leaving City

and the glittering future in store at Rovers, but Craig let it all wash over him, waiting for the moment when he could bring himself to say something. He'd been too stunned to do it on the drive home from the Flynns' house yesterday evening, but now he felt ready. A small, hot spot of anger was swiftly growing deep inside him.

'This car is yours really, isn't it, Dad?' he said suddenly, interrupting his father. 'And you needn't bother to deny it, either. Wayne Flynn told me.'

'Oh, did he?' said Craig's dad, frowning. 'How does Wayne know that?'

'You told his dad about how you talked the salesman into giving you a sweet deal,' said Craig, 'and he told Davy in front of Wayne. Big mouths are obviously a feature of the Flynn family. Mr Flynn was impressed, but I'm not,' he added, and paused. 'Why did you lie to me, Dad?' he asked, quietly.

'Look, Craig,' said Dad, smiling at him as they left the darkness of the country behind them and entered a lit suburban street, 'I was only thinking of you. Your mum was bound to ask you about the car, and if I'd told you the truth she would have wanted to know where I got the money for it, and there would have been the usual argy-bargy, and she might even have tried to stop me being involved with your football. And we don't want that, do we, son?'

'I suppose that's why you didn't tell me the other stuff, too,' said Craig. His dad glanced at him, but didn't say anything. 'Yeah, I know about you being in trouble because some deal has gone wrong,' Craig went on, 'and you owing somebody dodgy a lot of money. You told Mr Flynn that as well.'

'I didn't want to worry you,' said his dad smoothly. 'It's just grown-up stuff, problems I have to handle. Besides, I'll soon get it sorted, you'll see.'

'No you won't,' Craig hissed fiercely, that burning point of anger flaring into a flame inside him, 'because I won't be leaving City. So you won't be getting a bung from John Vulpine, or from Rovers, or from anyone else. Wayne told me how it works, how it might be as much as forty thousand quid, with more to come. And how that's the only thing you're interested in, *Dad*. I should have known from the start you were never interested in *me*.'

'Now listen, Craig, that's not true . . .' his dad began, but Craig simply ignored him. Eventually they pulled up at Craig's block, and Craig got out into the cold night air. 'Craig, don't go off like this . . .' his dad said.

But Craig walked away without a backward glance.

TWENTY

Friday was good and bad for Darren. Good because he was basking in the glow of being made captain, although when he'd woken up that morning it wasn't until his mum had popped her head round his door and said, 'Rise and shine, skipper!' that he'd realized he hadn't dreamt it. But bad too, because he had something to worry about – Craig, and what he might or might not do.

Darren couldn't help feeling guilty, too, remembering how he had almost betrayed his friend. During the day at school – when he wasn't drawing team formations and diagrams of set-piece line-ups in his rough book – he went over in his mind the conversation he'd had with Craig the night before, and decided he couldn't leave it there. Not now he was captain, anyway.

So that evening, as soon as he got in from school, Darren phoned Craig. It was ages before Craig answered, and when he did, he was very aggressive. Darren was amazed at how much anger Craig could put in the word 'Hello?'

'Hey, steady on, Craig,' said Darren. 'It's only me, mate.'

'Sorry, Daz,' said Craig. 'I thought you might be my dad.'

'But you get on OK with him, don't you?' Darren asked.

'I used to . . .' said Craig, and sighed. 'I don't any more.'

'What's happened then?' said Darren, and Craig told him the lot. Darren listened, amazed, to the story Wayne had told Craig, a tale of serious money changing hands before Davy Flynn left his former club – not that anybody could prove a thing, John Vulpine and Mr Flynn making sure of that – and of Craig's dad being after something similar to get him out of a dodgy situation.

'Is it all true, though?' Darren asked at last. 'Maybe Motormouth is just trying to wind you up. You said you thought he was jealous of you.'

'Look, I don't know if any of the stuff about Davy is kosher,' said Craig. 'And Wayne said I wouldn't be worth as much as Davy anyway, what with me only being thirteen. But my dad obviously thought he could make a few quid out of me. So that's all I must mean to him. A chance to make money.'

Craig fell silent, and for a few seconds Darren didn't know what to say. He suddenly felt way out of his depth. He'd had friends in the past whose parents had got into messes of various kinds, even one mate at primary school whose dad had been sent to prison. But he'd never known anyone whose dad had tried to pull a stunt like this. Darren thought that suddenly discovering your dad was plotting to make money out of you must be a pretty major downer.

'So what are you going to do?' Darren asked. 'I mean, there's no problem if you've made your mind up to stay at City, is there? That's it, job done.'

'I don't know, Daz . . .' Craig said, quietly. 'I'm not sure if I can hack it at City any more. It was OK all the time I thought I had my dad behind me, but I can't see a whole lot of point in it now. I'm definitely not going to Rovers after all this, though, but I can't see myself at any other club, either. So I've actually been thinking of packing in the whole thing, hanging up my boots.'

'What, you mean give up the game?' said Darren, taken aback. This was something he hadn't expected. 'Not play football at all? You can't do that.'

'Why not?' said Craig, aggression returning to his voice.

'Because . . .' said Darren, thinking fast, 'because you're too bloody good to give it up, mate, and also because the team won't be the same without you. Come on, Craig . . . we need you. You will play tomorrow, won't you?'

There was silence on the line, and Darren held his breath, waiting.

'Yeah, I suppose so,' said Craig eventually. 'But I'll need a lift.'

'I'll ask my dad if you can come with us,' said Darren. 'I'm sure it'll be OK. What about your mum, though? Doesn't she want to take you?'

'She would if I asked her,' said Craig. 'But I don't want her to come. She totally blew her stack when I told her what Dad's been up to, and every time he phones she gives him a seriously hard time. He's been phoning a lot, too, but I won't talk to him, and I've got a feeling he might turn up at the game. And if my mum's there, well . . . I don't like to think what might happen.'

'I can see that,' said Darren, remembering another friend's birthday party and the spectacular row between divorcing parents that had wrecked it. The last thing Darren wanted was his best player being put off by any parental shenanigans on the touchline. 'We'll pick you up around nine, OK?' he said.

That was OK with Craig, and with Darren's dad. But when Darren went to bed later that night, those butterflies had returned to his stomach, and they were all wearing size fourteen football boots and kicking the hell out of each other. Darren finally dropped off, and woke early the next morning, still feeling anxious about his friend. He ate his breakfast without noticing what cereal was in his bowl, got washed and dressed, carefully packed his kitbag.

Then Gran and Grandad arrived, and it was time to leave. Darren hadn't realized till then, but his whole family was coming to watch him play.

'We wouldn't miss it for the world,' said Grandad. 'It's not every day you get to see the competitive debut of a centre-half who'll be a star a few years from now.' Grandad paused. Gran was frowning and shaking her head at him. 'Not that it matters if you aren't, of course,' Grandad added, hastily.

'I think what your grandfather is trying to say, Darren . . .' said Gran.

'It's OK, Gran,' said Darren, smiling. 'I know what he's trying to say.'

There were too many of them to fit into one car for the drive to Hawks' Nest, so Mum, Ashleigh and Gemma went with Gran and Grandad in the Focus, the girls dazed to be out at 8.30 on a cold autumn Saturday, Darren going with his dad in the van. The plan was to collect Craig on the way.

'You up for this then, son?' Darren's dad asked him after a while. The streets were almost empty of traffic except for milk floats and the odd bus.

'Yeah, I think so,' Darren replied, pulling down the screen visor to shield his eyes from the bright sun. 'I'll be fine once we're playing, anyway.'

'I'm sure you will be too,' said his dad. 'You know, Darren, we're very proud of you and the fact that you've achieved this by yourself. And listen, don't worry about that other stuff – the bills and the house and everything.'

'Why, is it all sorted?' Darren asked hopefully.

'Not quite,' said his dad. Darren glanced at him and saw he was frowning slightly. 'Although we're working on it. Your gran and grandad are lending us a few bob again, which is great. I just don't know what we would have done without them . . . but they haven't got an endless supply of money, and we can't depend on them for ever. So I've started looking for another job.'

'What kind of job?' asked Darren, the way his dad was talking to him making him feel strangely older somehow, almost as if they were equals.

'Any job that pays better,' said his dad. 'I've got no qualifications, so it won't be easy. But life isn't, is it? I've made up my mind, though. From now on *I* am going to take care of business,' he said, determined. 'OK, son?'

'OK, Dad,' said Darren, and the two of them smiled at each other.

They turned into a quiet street lined with parked cars, and stopped as near as they could to the address Craig had given Darren, a modern block of flats four storeys high, Grandad slipping into a space a bit further down. Darren looked up and saw Craig waving from a third-floor window. A moment later Craig emerged from the block and came over to them. Darren got out of the van, took his friend's kitbag from him, and chucked it in the back with his.

'Morning, Craig,' said Darren's dad as the two boys got in, Craig nodding and sitting next to him, Darren by the door. It was a tight squeeze, the lads both wearing big puffa jackets that hissed and crackled when they came into contact with each other. 'Pleased to meet you, anyway,' said Darren's dad, easing the van away from the kerb, Grandad following closely behind.

Darren glanced up at Craig's window, saw a woman there watching them leave, and realized it must be Craig's mum. Even at a distance he could see the resemblance. But he didn't say anything, and Craig didn't say much during the journey. Darren's dad tried to talk to him, but got nowhere.

Eventually, Dad glanced at Darren over Craig's head, raising his eyebrows as if to say, 'What's his problem?' Darren gave his dad an I've-Got-No-Idea shrug, hoping his dad would put Craig's mood down to pre-match nerves. His dad shrugged too and gave up at last, the journey continuing in silence.

'Here we are then,' said Darren's dad at last, turning through the wide-open gates and into Hawks' Nest. 'We're not the first to arrive, either.'

They stopped in the car park behind two other cars. One was a familiar silver Volvo estate, which wasn't any surprise, thought Darren, the gaffer always getting to the training ground early. But the other was a red Frontera, and there was Craig's dad standing beside it, smoking and staring at them.

Oh no, thought Darren, his heart sinking. This is all I need . . .

TWENTY-ONE

Craig had also seen his father, the instant they entered the car park, in fact, and his heart had suddenly seemed to lurch sideways. He had lowered his eyes as they parked behind the Frontera, unwilling to return his dad's gaze. The passenger door of the van was on the opposite side to where his dad was standing, and Craig got out after Darren, keeping his head down as they went to the rear of the van to fetch their kitbags. But there was no escape.

'All right, Craig?' said his dad, quickly coming round from his side. Craig still wouldn't look at him, taking his bag from Darren and heading towards the pavilion. 'Craig!' said his dad, slightly raising his voice. 'I'm beginning to think you're trying to avoid me, son,' he said, laughing uncomfortably for the benefit of the Kimbles. He flashed a dazzling smile at them, then turned his full attention back to Craig. 'I just want a word with you, that's all,' he said.

Craig realized his dad wasn't going to leave him alone, so he stopped.

'You OK, Craig?' said Darren uncertainly, stopping too, a concerned expression on his face, glancing from Craig to Craig's dad. Darren's dad was standing by the van, and Craig noticed he was frowning, obviously puzzled by what was going on. The rest of Darren's family were watching as well.

'Yeah, sure,' said Craig. He decided he didn't want an audience for what was about to happen. 'I'll see you inside,' he said. 'This won't take long.'

'Right,' said Darren. He reluctantly walked off and spoke to his family, Craig distinctly hearing Darren's dad say: 'What's all that about then?' but he didn't catch Darren's murmured reply. Then Darren headed for the pavilion, his family loudly calling out good luck to him, that they'd be on the touchline.

Craig waited, and his dad finally appeared before him.

'Listen, son,' Dad said, throwing down his cigarette and putting his hand on Craig's shoulder. 'I know you're upset, but you're making a big mistake.'

'Really?' Craig asked, staring coldly at Dad's hand as if it were some kind of alien creature. His dad took it away. 'Well, I don't think so,' Craig said.

'You shouldn't believe everything you hear,' said his dad, 'especially not from the Flynns. It's like you said, Wayne and his dad have got big mouths.'

'What are you saying, Dad?' asked Craig, looking into his eyes, thinking now they weren't like his own at all. 'That you *weren't* after some money? That you weren't going to make a killing out of me, out of your own *son*?'

'OK, Craig, I'll put my hand up to it,' said his dad, raising his right hand and grinning at him. 'I would have told you eventually, you know I would . . . Anyway, that's how the world works, son, so you'd better get used to it. You're a talented boy, and plenty more people are going to try and make a few quid from you over the next few years. So why don't we keep it in the family? I can still look out for your best interests at the same time, can't I?'

'Don't give me that crap,' said Craig, bitterly. 'Keep it in the *family*? You don't know what that word means. I should have listened to Mum. She says the only person you've ever looked out for is yourself, and she's right.'

'Yeah, well, that's what I'd expect your mother to say,' said Dad, his eyes narrowed, his lips tight, his whole face suddenly taking on a mean look. And underneath that, Craig realized, there was something else . . . fear.

'Is that all you've got to say, then?' Craig asked, tight-lipped himself.

'No, it isn't,' said his dad, changing tack, moving closer, making his voice quieter, more intimate. 'Look, Craig, I don't mind admitting I need to come up with some cash, so you'd definitely be doing your old man a favour if you went to Rovers. But it really is a great opportunity, and besides, there might even be a couple of grand in it for you . . . Think what you could buy with that.'

Craig froze, hardly able to believe what he'd just heard, his own father actually trying to buy him off with a couple of thousand pounds. He could see a strained eagerness to persuade him in his dad's face, hear an uncool edge of desperation in his pleading voice. It was like looking at a total stranger, Craig thought suddenly, someone he had never known. But that was the truth, he realized. His father *was* a stranger to him, and had never been anything else.

'So, you're offering to cut me in on the deal, is that it?' Craig asked.

'Yeah, sure, son,' said his father, smiling again. 'Whatever you want.'

'I just don't believe this,' said Craig. 'It's not about money, it's about . . .' He paused, his eyes prickling as he tried to express what he felt inside. But he couldn't find the words. 'I'll tell you what I want, Dad,' he said at last. 'I want you to get lost, now. And I never, ever want to see you again.'

Then he turned on his heel and walked away, his dad saying something, Craig ignoring him and heading straight for the pavilion, the car park behind him beginning to fill with more cars. Craig banged through the pavilion doors, realized his eyes were wet, and if he didn't get himself under control he might start crying like a baby. Which wouldn't do much for his reputation.

He ducked into the toilets. They were empty, luckily. He dropped his bag on the concrete floor, ran cold water into one of the basins, plunged his face into its soothing, wet blankness. Then he straightened up, took several deep breaths, examined himself in a mirror. He looked OK, he thought, drying himself with paper towels, picking up his bag again. Not great, but OK.

Craig slipped out and joined the lads heading past the gym and the physio suite, quietly

returning their greetings, staying silent otherwise. The lads filed into the usual changing
room, but as Craig reached it, the gaffer came
from the direction of his office, accompanied
by four other adults – Roy Newton, Mike Wilmot
and two men Craig didn't recognize, the gaffer
and Mike Wilmot in City coaching staff jackets,
the others in expensive coats.

'Hang on a second, Craig,' said the gaffer, and
Craig paused. 'I'd like you to meet some people.
You know Roy, of course, but I don't think
you've been properly introduced to Mike, and
these two gentlemen are from our sponsors.
Kevin Laws is MD of QuickPhone UK, and Jan
Brondby is head of the Danish parent company.
And this, gentlemen, is Craig Hurst.'

Kevin Laws was tall and greying and looked a
little overweight, Jan Brondby younger and even
taller, with thick blond hair swept back from a
broad forehead. Each shook hands with Craig, as
did Roy and Mike Wilmot.

'I've been hearing good things about you,
Craig,' said Mike Wilmot, smiling at him.
'Jimmy here's been telling me you're a natural
striker . . . and if there's one kind of player you
need at any club, it's a reliable goal-scorer.'

'Especially if you can get him for free, eh?' said
Kevin Laws. 'What's the going rate for a reason-

able striker these days, Mike? Five million? Ten?'

'That much and a bit more,' said Mike Wilmot. 'For someone with real class you're probably not going to get much change out of fifteen big ones.'

'There you are, Craig,' said Jan Brondby, his English faintly accented. 'You could be in the first team in a few years, worth that much yourself.'

'Never mind a few years,' said Mike Wilmot, 'if he does well today, I might play him in the first team next week. We need a good goal-scorer.'

The men laughed, showing their teeth, and Craig wondered what Joe Johnson might think if he'd heard what Mike Wilmot had said. Then he decided he didn't care, his mood sinking even lower, a black hole opening inside him and everything tumbling into it. Was his dad right? Was this how it was going to be, everybody seeing pound signs when they looked at him?

'Anyway, best of luck, Craig,' said Roy Newton. 'See you later.'

Roy, Mike, Kevin Laws and Jan Brondby moved off down the corridor, but the gaffer hung back and stood beside Craig, blocking his path into the changing room. The rest of the squad had turned up now, and were in there getting changed. Craig knew what was coming, felt uncomfortable.

'You OK, Craig?' said the gaffer, his eyes boring into him. Craig looked down, unable to meet his coach's searching gaze. 'I thought you didn't seem happy at training on Thursday, and your mood obviously hasn't improved since. Anything you want to talk about? Everything all right at home?'

'Yeah, gaffer,' said Craig, trying to keep his voice neutral. 'Er . . . I mean, no, there's nothing I want to talk about, and everything at home is fine.'

'I'm glad to hear it,' said the gaffer, not sounding too convinced. 'But just remember, son – my door is always open. Now in you go and get changed.'

The gaffer moved aside, and Craig ducked into the noisy changing room, dropped his kitbag on the floor and sat on the bench in the space Darren had saved for him. He leaned forward and covered his face with his hands.

'You OK, Twink?' Darren whispered, his voice full of concern.

'Why does everyone keep asking me that?' Craig snapped. He jumped up and pulled off his jacket, then savagely unzipped his kitbag.

And that black hole inside him was getting bigger all the time.

TWENTY-TWO

Darren felt even more worried now about Craig's state of mind, but decided his friend was probably best left to himself for the time being. There wasn't much he could do or say to Craig in a crowded changing room anyway, so he carried on getting changed into his kit, pulled on his boots and laced them up. Most of the other lads were ready, Craig having been the last one into the changing room, and the noise was slowly beginning to subside.

The banter had been different today, thought Darren, much less cruel than usual, and edgier, shot through with an excitement you could almost see crackling in the atmosphere of the changing room. This was the squad's big moment, their first competitive game for City FC, and most of them seemed to have realized they were in it together. Even the substitutes, the lads who hadn't made the starting eleven, seemed pumped-up, full of anticipation.

Everyone was raring to go, thought Darren. Everyone except Craig.

Darren pulled on his tracksuit top and trousers and sat back down on the bench, his stomach churning, his legs trembling slightly. He glanced round at Craig, who had changed too. He wondered what had gone on in the car park, what Craig's dad could have said to make Craig even more unhappy than he had been before. Darren tried to think of something *he* could say to turn things round, make Craig focus on the game, but his mind was a blank.

Then the gaffer strode in, and everybody turned their attention to him.

'All right, lads, listen up,' he said, standing next to the whiteboard, Des and Andy behind him in the doorway. The room fell into silence, and the gaffer scanned their faces before he continued. 'A few words on what kind of opposition we're likely to be facing this morning,' he said. 'I haven't seen them play, and they might only be a second division club, but I can guarantee any side Tony Rosemount puts out will be hard to beat . . .'

The gaffer told them how Tony Rosemount

believed good teams were built on rock-solid defence, that he taught his lads to pressure their opponents' first touch and never to let them settle or develop a rhythm. His teams tended to pack the midfield, snuffing out attacks before they got going, pressing into the final third of the pitch and always looking for defenders to make mistakes. Then they would come at you fast, getting plenty of bodies into the box.

'Now I think Tony will play three at the back, as per usual,' said the gaffer, quickly outlining half a pitch on the whiteboard with a marker pen and using small 'X's to represent the Warlington players, 'with two wing-backs to cover the flanks, four across the middle, and a single target man upfront. It's not pretty, but it can be effective, especially if they rattle you early on. So how do we counter this kind of formation? What do you think, Darren?'

The gaffer turned that penetrating stare of his on Darren, who hadn't been expecting to be asked a question. Everybody in the room was looking at Darren now, waiting for him to reply, and for a second he felt rattled himself. Then he saw the gaffer smiling at him, and suddenly he knew the answer.

'We make sure . . . we don't panic,' he said, smiling back at the gaffer, feeling as if he'd scored top marks in a test. His legs stopped trembling, too.

'Spot on,' said the gaffer, giving him a little wink, making him feel there was a special bond between them. 'We . . . don't . . . panic. We stay patient, we keep possession, we pass the ball well, we make *them* do all the running and tire themselves out in the process, and we wait for the gaps to appear. We've got two great strikers in Wayne and Craig, and if we can get them a couple of half chances, then Bob is probably our uncle. Everybody OK with that?'

There was a general murmur of agreement from the lads, most of whom seemed slightly less tense now. Darren glanced at Craig, who was leaning back against the clothes hanging from his peg, arms folded, eyes on Wayne, his expression impossible to read. Wayne – who had been very quiet so far – briefly returned Craig's stare, his expression uneasy, then looked away.

Oh, great, thought Darren, his heart sinking. These two are supposed to win the game for us, and they're probably not even speaking to each other.

'And one last thing, boys,' said the gaffer. 'Remember, this is a team game. So play for each other out there, OK? Now . . . let's go to work.'

The lads jumped to their feet and started

bustling through the door, a thunderous sound of studs clattering on the concrete floor, everybody except Wayne, Craig and Darren laughing and joking loudly, some clapping others on the shoulder, wishing them the best of luck for the game. Darren followed them out, but the gaffer put his hand lightly on Darren's arm, held him back.

'I'm a bit worried about Craig,' said the gaffer quietly, letting Darren move on again, walking with him. They went past the physio suite and the gym together, the rest of the lads in front of them. 'He's not really himself at the moment,' he went on. 'We'd better both keep an eye on him, and if things aren't going well, we'll pull him off, bring on a sub. OK with you, Darren?'

'Yeah, sure, boss,' said Darren, half pleased to be consulted, half nervously wondering what the gaffer knew or had guessed. 'No problem.'

'Good,' said the gaffer as they went outside. 'Got a few VIPs watching us today,' he murmured, nodding towards two groups of men meeting in the car park. Darren recognized Mike Wilmot, and realized the others must be club directors and people from QuickPhone. 'So we could do with a result. A win wouldn't do our funding any harm . . .' The gaffer paused. 'Anyway, it's a fine day for a game,' he said. 'Off you go, son. Remember – relax and enjoy it.'

That was easier said than done, thought Darren, trotting onto the near pitch where Des and Andy were already taking the lads through the usual warm-up routine, the knowledge of who would be watching adding to the pressure he was already feeling. But the gaffer was right, it *was* a fine day for a game. The sun was shining in a clear blue sky, and there was no wind to speak of. It was chilly, but not too cold, and the pitch was firm and dry, the line-markings freshly white-washed, the City FC corner flags in position.

'Seen the opposition?' muttered Paul as Darren joined the circle and started doing his hamstring stretches. 'They look like right hard-nuts.'

'They're probably saying the same thing about us,' said Jamie. 'I mean, some of them might look tasty, but we've got Drew and Lee, remember?'

Darren glanced beyond him and saw another group of tracksuited boys doing a similar warm-up routine. Jamie was right, Drew and Lee did look menacing, but a couple of the opposition players were pretty big, and one in particular – a tall, fair, raw-boned lad with huge hands and feet – had a definite Don't-Mess-With-Me air about him. Darren wondered if he was an attacker or a defender, and thought he'd be a handful wherever he played.

Two men in tracksuits were with the Warlington lads, a black guy with a very familiar face, and a thickset, older white man with a full head of dark, curly hair. Darren recognized the younger man as a Liverpool player until last season, and realized he must have gone into coaching. Then he glimpsed the initials TR on the older man's top, and knew he was Tony Rosemount.

It was odd, thought Darren – Tony Rosemount didn't look a bit like the gaffer, but there were definite similarities, Tony Rosemount giving the same impression of calmness and experience that made whatever the gaffer said so compelling. Which probably meant the Warlington team had been well coached: City were in for a real game.

There was a larger crowd of spectators on the touchlines today too, Darren noticed. Most of the dads who came regularly to training were there, along with some mums and brothers and sisters and grandparents, and quite a few people Darren didn't recognize. Mike Wilmot and the VIPs had taken up a position near halfway, and were laughing loudly at each other's jokes.

Standing near them was Craig's dad with Mr

Flynn, the two of them talking to each other, neither of them looking happy. Darren glanced across at Craig and Wayne, but both were concentrating on their warm-ups and didn't seem to be paying any attention to their fathers. Darren hoped that's how it would stay once the game actually kicked off, but had a feeling it wouldn't.

Then Darren saw the referee walking onto the pitch with his assistants, the three of them in official kit as if this was a professional game. Des and Andy brought the warm-up to a close and the lads all went over to the touchline where the gaffer was standing. They stripped off their tracksuits, the gaffer getting them to do a little ball work while Darren went up for the coin-toss.

Darren waved to his family as he jogged out to the centre circle, and they waved back. It was good to know they were there for him, but his dad was right, Darren thought proudly. He *had* made it this far on his own efforts . . .

And suddenly Darren knew exactly what to say to Craig.

TWENTY-THREE

Craig watched Darren in the centre circle, the red and black of Darren's City shirt a strong contrast with the yellow strip of the Warlington captain facing him. Craig looked down at his own City shirt, gently touching the raised gold crest over his heart. It was strange, he thought. He'd been dreaming of a moment like this for years, and it just didn't seem to matter any more.

But then nothing seemed to matter any more. Nothing at all.

He didn't know now why he had let Darren persuade him to play today. It seemed totally pointless to him, and football itself a strange, stupid activity, twenty-two boys chasing a ball round a muddy field while a bunch of other people stood watching, shouting at them and getting themselves worked up.

Craig looked along the touchline to where

his father was talking to Ron Flynn, and just then the two men suddenly turned to stare at him. Craig looked away, remembering how badly he had once wanted his dad to come and watch him play, to be there for him like a proper father. Now he wished Dad would get in that flashy Frontera and drive out of his life for ever.

The referee was in the centre circle as well, flanked by his two assistants, and Craig saw him flipping a coin, the captains leaning over and peering as it landed on the short grass. Craig saw Darren smile and shake hands with the Warlington skipper, then turn and summon the City team onto the pitch. The lads around Craig broke into a run, and Craig followed them slowly.

'Come on you Hawks!' he heard somebody yell behind him, and other voices calling out, some for Warlington, and loud whistling and clapping. Craig reached the centre circle, where the referee was quickly checking everybody's studs before the teams got into position for the kick-off. That done at last, Craig took up his position by the ball on the centre spot.

Standing next to him was Wayne Flynn. Beyond them the referee was studying his wristwatch, obviously waiting for it to show precisely 10.30.

'Listen, Craig,' said Wayne quietly, 'whatever you think of me, I had my reasons, OK? And it was better for you to know what your dad was up to.'

Craig was surprised Wayne was trying to justify his actions, Wayne's face showing his usual aggressiveness, but mixed with a guilt he couldn't hide.

'Oh yeah?' said Craig, staring at Wayne coldly until he looked down. 'I don't usually hold grudges. But in your case I think I'll make an exception.'

Wayne seemed to want to say something else, but didn't get the chance.

'All right, skippers?' the referee called out, the Warlington captain and Darren both raising their hands to show their teams were ready. Then the referee checked with his assistants on the touchlines, gave a long, loud blast on his whistle, waved his arms in a forward motion . . . and the game began.

Wayne tapped the ball to Craig, who swept it back without even looking, guessing Curtis was somewhere behind him. Wayne was already heading down the left side channel, making straight for the Warlington box, calling for a ball from midfield, and Craig realized he should be doing the same on the right. He started running, but his legs were like lead, and he soon stopped.

He turned and looked downfield, a familiar numbness making him feel as if somehow he wasn't really there. Craig saw Curtis pick up his loose pass and lay it off to Ben, who controlled the ball and quickly brought it upfield. The gaffer had been dead right about Warlington's tactics, thought Craig, two opposition midfield players immediately coming in to close Ben down.

But Ben knocked a sweet ball out to Jamie, the latter moving at pace and taking it perfectly in his stride, pushing it past an opposition midfielder and galloping off towards the byline. Craig could see the whole yellow defence swivelling in that direction and he felt his legs twitch, his football instincts sensing the attacking possibilities, his body responding against his will.

Craig set off, his feet taking him into a space between the Warlington midfield coming back in support and their rearmost three defenders. He glimpsed Wayne and Curtis in the box, both looking for Jamie to put in a cross, Jason moving up as well. But as Craig arrived on the edge of the area, Jamie suddenly cut inside the wing-back, totally wrong-footing the defence.

Then Jamie rolled a beautiful, perfect pass across the corner of the box and into Craig's path. Craig looked up, saw a clear shot on goal, glimpsed the panic on the out-of-position Warlington keeper's face . . . and fluffed it, over-running the ball so he couldn't hit it first time, a raw-boned, fair-haired central defender booting it clear and clattering into him simultaneously.

Craig went down face first, his arms and chest jarring on the ground. He rolled over and sat up, hearing someone shout an appeal to the ref for a foul, seeing the ref shake his head and wave play on, the defender's clearance dropping into the City half. Craig got to his feet and made his way back, Jamie looking at him confused, the defender who'd clattered him smirking.

'Come on, Craig, you can do better than that!' somebody yelled from the touchline. It sounded like Des, but Craig didn't turn round or acknowledge the comment, even though he knew it was correct. He felt himself blushing, embarrassed, and hated the idea that he might make a fool of himself in front of the crowd, maybe allow his dad to think the money thing had got to him.

But it *had* got to him, Craig thought. It had got to him big time.

Craig shook his head and tried to concentrate on the game, realizing City were in possession again, Drew controlling the ball, Ben coming to him to take it and launch another attack. But the Warlington midfield surrounded Ben, making a square ball to Lee on the left his only real option unless he went for a route one hit-and-hope. But Ben just wasn't a route one kind of player, and as Craig reached the halfway line, Ben slipped the ball to Lee.

Craig stopped, sensing someone behind him. He looked round, and the fair-haired defender was practically breathing down his neck, giving him the stare, the one that says, 'Come and have a go if you think you're hard enough'.

Craig stared back to show he wasn't intimidated, then slowly turned away. But the defender followed, pressing a shoulder into the back of Craig's arm.

'You ain't seen nothing yet,' said the defender, laughing. 'Loser,' he added, his face contorted with contempt, almost spitting the word at Craig.

Meanwhile, two yellow-shirted midfielders were closing Lee down, and he was looking to pass the ball. Jason called for it inside, and Lee shipped it on to him, Jason then moving it to Wayne. Craig made for the Warlington box, the fair-haired defender keeping pace with him, bumping his shoulder again, jockeying him, tugging at his shirt, nearly knocking Craig off-balance.

But that attack petered out, as did the next one, and the next, the game soon settling into a rhythm of City winning possession and launching forays into the Warlington half, Warlington pressing through the middle of the park, harrying City players on the ball, blocking every route forward. The midfield grafted busily, Wayne bustled, but nothing seemed to produce any results.

And for Craig it was a strange game, his legs still feeling heavy, his mind fuzzy. His touch seemed to have gone completely, and he made a mess of every ball that came to him. Not that it would have mattered anyway, he thought, that same defender tracking him everywhere, harassing him into mistakes, making sure he stayed the right side of fouling him. But only just.

Craig began to feel frustrated, the groans from the City supporters when he failed to control a pass or mis-timed a run making him blush again, the laughter and catcalls from Warlington parents adding to his embarrassment. And that defender kept nipping at his ankles, tugging his shirt, pushing him.

Then Craig snapped, and pushed him back on the edge of the Warlington box, the defender falling over with a look of pain and outraged innocence on his face. The ref dashed across, gave a free kick, called Craig over to him.

Craig approached the ref slowly, everyone else – players and spectators – suddenly falling strangely quiet, waiting to see what the ref was going to do.

'I don't want to see that kind of behaviour, young man,' said the ref, who was thin, balding, beaky-nosed. He took a small notebook out of his shirt pocket, wrote Craig's number in it, then pulled a yellow card from inside the notebook and held it up. 'Any more trouble and you'll be off,' he said.

Craig was stunned, barely registering the boos from the touchline, the Warlington physio running on to minister to the fair-haired defender who was still on the ground, pretending his leg was injured, trying to make it look as bad as possible. It was the first time Craig had ever been booked . . . and suddenly he felt that hot spot of anger wink on inside him once more.

He turned to head for his own half, head down, his face burning. Then he glimpsed something from the corner of his eye that made him stop dead.

His mum was on the touchline, striding towards his dad.

TWENTY-FOUR

Darren saw Craig's mum arrive too, and hurried from his place on the edge of the City area to speak to his friend, realizing the stoppage might be the only chance he would get to say his piece. As he jogged up the pitch, Darren glanced at the gaffer on the touchline. The gaffer was looking steadily at Darren, head tilted and eyebrows raised, his meaning patently clear.

But Darren already knew that Craig was running out of time.

That yellow card might make things very difficult. Warlington were proving a pretty tough nut to crack, and Darren had the feeling they were more than capable of resisting the City pressure, then pinching a goal from a breakaway. He could also see Craig was having a battle with the fair-haired defender, and knew any more retaliation might earn him a red card. Then City would be down to ten with their best goal-scorer back in the changing room.

Not that Craig was showing any form, thought Darren. In fact, he'd been totally off the pace, a passenger, practically the whole City side – Wayne included – working their socks off to provide him with the ball and let him do his stuff, then having to watch him arrive late, stumble, lose possession. It was painful to see, and Darren felt deeply for his friend. But perhaps what he was going to say now might do the trick. Darren certainly hoped it would.

'Come on, Craig,' said Darren, approaching Craig in the centre circle. Craig was standing still, his gaze fixed on the touchline. Darren looked in the same direction, and saw that Craig's parents seemed to be arguing intensely, although it was obviously Craig's mum doing most of the talking, punctuating what she said with lots of angry gestures. Darren looked away, stood in front of Craig. 'You're going to have to pull yourself together, mate,' he said.

'That's easy for you to say,' muttered Craig, turning to face him. Darren could hear the sharp edge of anger in his friend's voice, see it glitter in his narrowed eyes. 'It's a lot harder to do, though,' said Craig.

'Maybe,' said Darren shrugging. 'It still

happens to be the truth. You're letting the gaffer and the lads down, and that's bang out of order. I know it's not your fault, but they don't. And you're the only one who can sort it.'

'Oh yeah?' said Craig, his cheeks flushing. 'Any suggestions, then?'

'Just the one,' said Darren. 'Forget about your dad. You don't need him, and you never have done, not as far as football is concerned, anyway. You got this far on your own, Craig. That's all you have to remember.'

Craig stared at him, his brow furrowed, seemingly surprised by what Darren had just said. Darren glanced upfield, saw the Warlington physio leaving the pitch, the fair-haired defender up on his feet again, the keeper getting ready to take the free kick, sneaking an extra couple of metres, moving the ball forward while the ref's attention was directed elsewhere.

'Daz, I . . .' Craig began to say, but Darren cut him off.

'Later,' he said, 'we don't have time for this right now.'

And with that, Darren ran back to his position in defence, nodding at the gaffer on the way, noticing that Craig's mum and dad had stopped arguing, Craig's mum standing on the touchline alone, facing the pitch, hands in the pockets of her raincoat, Craig's dad walking towards his car. Then the free kick was taken, and the City captain had to focus on the game once more.

The ball went short to a Warlington wing-back, who pushed it on to a team-mate, Darren calling for his fellow defenders to move up and squeeze the midfield, but not going too far in case they left themselves open to a through ball, or a chip over the top for a runner to catch them square. But neither happened, Warlington playing across the park, keeping possession.

Then a Warlington midfielder tried a long ball, aiming at their sole target man, a medium-sized kid who looked pretty useful, even if he hadn't had much service so far. But Drew easily intercepted the pass, laying the ball off to Paul immediately. Paul took it to the byline, gave it to Jamie, and Jamie drilled it hard first time through a crowd of players towards Craig.

Darren had moved upfield, and watched anxiously as Craig shaped to take the pass, the fair-haired defender quickly coming in to jostle him from behind.

But Craig took a good first touch and stayed on his feet, holding off the defender, then laid the ball back to Ben, who was coming up fast from the centre circle. Ben dummied to pass to Wayne for a wall ball, then thumped in a crisp, grass-cutting shot instead, forcing the Warlington keeper to make a save. He went down to his right, gratefully gathering the ball to his chest.

'That's more like it, City!' Darren heard somebody in the crowd yelling, and a scattering of applause. Darren retreated, automatically checking the positions of his fellow defenders and the yellow-shirted players in front of him, relieved that Craig had managed to do something half-decent at last.

The Warlington keeper rolled the ball to one of his defenders, and the game resumed its former pattern. But Darren soon noticed a difference. Craig did seem to have regained something of his touch, and was starting to play with more of his usual sharpness, and that was giving City more confidence.

Curtis put in a blistering low shot the Warlington keeper had to turn round the bottom of a post, then Drew went up for a corner and shaved the crossbar with a header. Suddenly City seemed to be hitting their stride, making good runs, passes going to feet, the opposition beginning to look shaky, even panicky, the crowd picking up the change and getting noisy and excited.

As his team piled on the pressure, Darren

stayed just inside his own half, wanting to make sure the defence was anchored, that they weren't taken by surprise. And then, when everybody but Darren and Sam behind him were in the Warlington area for yet another City corner . . . they very nearly were.

Jamie whipped in a beautiful out-swinger, but a big Warlington defender nodded it to safety. It fell to a yellow-shirted midfielder on the edge of the box, and he quickly took it forward a few metres, beating Ben and Paul, then rolled it up to his target man, who swivelled . . . and came straight at Darren.

The target man took one touch, then another, and Darren started to back-pedal at an angle, hoping to force the Warlington player to the byline where he could probably close him down without too much trouble. But the target man wasn't having any of it, and knocked the ball beyond him, flying past at pace, Darren having to turn and chase, the crowd exploding into yells.

Darren was three metres short of his man and had to put on a real spurt to catch him. In the distance he could see Sam moving up to narrow the angle like the good keeper he was. But Darren knew that any goalie is at a disadvantage in a one-on-one with a striker bearing down on him fast. So he decided he'd have to take responsibility, make the tackle himself.

Timing, timing, timing, he thought, blocking out the touchline noise, hearing only his own breathing and the thudding of his boots and those of his opponent on the turf, seeing the Warlington player suddenly glance at him over his shoulder, a flash of worry on his face. The target man accelerated away, Darren suddenly having to find even more speed to keep up with him.

The City box was just five metres ahead when Darren made his move. He concentrated on the ball, remembering a great tackle he'd seen in a video, Bobby Moore taking the ball off Pelé's feet, and he leapt forward, right leg extended, making sure he didn't foul the attacker but getting his foot over the ball, bringing it to a dead stop, going down, but getting to his feet and quickly taking the ball upfield and out of the danger zone. The Warlington player had fallen on the edge of the box too, and appealed loudly for a penalty.

But the ref shook his head, waved play on, and Darren tuned in to the touchline, suddenly hearing the yelling, the cheers and clapping, smiling as Drew called out, 'Great tackle, Daz!' Darren slipped the ball to Jamie, glimpsed his family waving madly at him, and nodded briefly to them. Then he gave his fellow defenders a right rollocking, and got on with the game.

Half-time came sooner than Darren expected, both sides trooping off through the applauding crowd to their changing rooms. The gaffer got the lads in, sat them down, checked for knocks, made sure they all had a drink, then went over the first-half performance, pointing out any problems, getting feedback, telling them things about the opposition he'd spotted. Darren was relieved to see Craig definitely seemed less wound-up, and so did Wayne.

Then it was time for the team to go back out again, and off they went.

'Nice tackle, Darren,' the gaffer said quietly to him as they went outside. 'But then I always knew I could rely on you. And whatever you said to Craig seems to have hit the spot . . . so we'll leave things as they are, OK?'

'OK, boss,' Darren replied, feeling ten feet tall.

He just couldn't wait for the second half to begin.

TWENTY-FIVE

Craig trotted out with the other lads, then stopped on the touchline, waiting for the gaffer and Darren to catch up. The referee and his assistants were just emerging from the changing rooms themselves, and weren't hurrying to the pitch, so Craig decided he had time to do what he had to before the kick-off.

But he thought he ought to talk to the gaffer first, explain the booking.

'Sorry about the card, boss,' he said as the gaffer and Darren approached. 'That big defender was just snapping at me from the off, and I finally lost it.'

'Not to worry, Craig,' said the gaffer. He and Darren stopped. 'Between you and me I thought the ref was a bit harsh,' he commented, 'but I hope it's taught you a lesson. It's an old rule, son. He who retaliates loses, especially if you do it in front of the ref. You need to keep your cool, try taking the lad on, turn him inside out a few times. He might be strong, but he's not quick.'

'I will, boss,' said Craig, seeing that the gaffer's suggestion was a good one. 'Is it OK if I have a word with my mum quickly?' he asked.

'Sure, no problem, son,' said the gaffer, smiling at him. 'So long as you promise me a terrific second-half performance, that is. How about it?'

'I'll do my best,' said Craig, returning his smile.

'That's good enough for me,' said the gaffer, nodding at him, 'and it's all I'll ever expect. You've got a couple of minutes,' he said, and walked away.

Darren hung back, and the two friends stood in silence for a moment.

'You going to be OK, Twink?' Darren asked him at last.

'I'm sorted, Daz,' Craig replied. 'Thanks for the advice.'

'Part of the service, mate,' said Darren, grinning broadly, then turning and running onto the pitch. Craig headed down the touchline, through the noisy crowd, making for his mum. She saw him coming, and they met halfway.

Craig looked at her in the cold sunshine, at her neat blond hair, her green eyes, her smart black raincoat, and he suddenly realized Darren hadn't been quite right. Maybe he *had* never needed his dad, Craig thought, but he hadn't got this far entirely by his own efforts. Somebody else had always been there, somebody he could always rely on. He just hadn't appreciated what she'd been doing for him before. And not just with his football, either.

'If that big blond boy kicks you once more, I'll come out there and kick *him*,' said his mum fiercely. 'I can't believe he's being allowed to get away with it. Maybe I ought to give the referee a piece of my mind, too.'

'Whoa, steady on, Mum,' said Craig, laughing, but looking round to make sure the referee or his assistants hadn't heard her. 'You'll probably get us both sent off, and that won't do much for the old family reputation, will it?'

'Yes, well, I suppose I'll have to get used to all this awful macho stuff,' said his mum, 'seeing as I'll be coming regularly to watch you train and play from now on. But don't panic. I'll be sure to wear trousers at all times.'

Craig glanced down and saw his mum was wearing jeans tucked into the wellies she had bought him for his school trip last year, and he smiled. 'That's OK, then,' he said. 'What did you say to Dad?'

'Quite a lot,' said his mum. 'Most of it totally unprintable.'

'Really?' said Craig, pleased. 'Listen, Mum . . . I'm sorry.'

'What for?' she said. 'None of it was your fault, Craig.'

'No, I suppose it wasn't,' said Craig. 'Anyway, I have to go.'

'I know,' she said. 'See you later.' Craig ran onto the pitch, but his mum suddenly called out, 'Hang on, Craig!' and he stopped. Some of the City lads were within hearing distance, and Craig felt very uncomfortable, wondering if his mum might be on the point of seriously embarrassing him by saying something soppy in front of them, or worse, calling him 'love'. But she didn't. 'Give 'em hell, son,' she said, and smiled. Craig laughed again, then ran on.

He took his position on the edge of the centre circle between Wayne and Curtis, and waited for Warlington to kick off. The referee checked with his assistants and the captains, gave a blast on his whistle, and the second half began, Craig soon realizing that it looked like being more of the same. If anything, Warlington seemed to want to play it even tighter than before.

In fact, for the opening ten minutes of the half, Warlington harassed City continually, yellow shirts chasing everything, even lost causes, buzzing all round every City player on the ball, raising the pace, geeing each other up. Watching Warlington try to take the game by the scruff of the neck, Craig thought Tony Rosemount must have given his lads some half-time talk.

But City didn't crack, and Craig began to understand that he was part of a very good team, that his mates *were* playing for each other, doing what the gaffer had said, keeping it simple, staying patient, not getting rattled – even Wayne. And Craig knew now that he couldn't let them down any more.

The numbness had gone, and he'd buried any feelings he still had for his dad very deep, telling himself that's where they'd stay. He felt good, he felt cool, he felt ready to do the stuff he knew he could do. And he was ready now to take on that defender like the gaffer had said, make his life a misery.

His first opportunity came when a Warlington attack broke down, and Darren cleared the ball to Ben. Ben made a strong run through the middle of the park and laid the ball off to Craig, who'd dropped back, Ben running on into the box, calling for a quick return. But Craig ignored him, stopped dead.

The fair-haired defender came out to hustle him, a cocky grin on his face, obviously convinced Craig posed no major threat. Craig took a touch, moved forward, tempting the defender in . . . then stopped again, dragged the ball back with his right foot and spun off to the left, leaving his marker for dead.

Warlington were a well-organized side, so two other defenders instantly barred his way ahead, and Craig had no option but a square ball to Curtis for a shot that went wide. The crowd liked what Craig had done, though, and he felt even better seeing the cocky grin vanish from his tormentor's face.

'What was it you said?' asked Craig, laughing as he ran past. 'Oh yeah, I remember now. You ain't seen nothing yet. Well, watch this . . . loser.'

From then on it was the fair-haired defender's turn to feel frustrated. Craig sought him out, stuck with him, called for the ball as often as he could, and went through his whole repertoire of tricks every time he got it. He did drag-backs, Cruyff turns, feinted this way, that way, took the defender on runs, changed pace, stopped, started, stepped over the ball, nutmegged him.

And Craig never lost possession, always making sure that he finished with a good lay-off, a decent cross or shot. The crowd loved it, all the City lads loved it, Craig loved it. The fair-haired defender absolutely hated it, lunging at Craig, chasing him, totally losing his cool . . . and eventually hacking him down with a clumsy challenge that drew loud booing from the touch-line.

'You OK?' said one of Craig's team-mates, helping him to his feet.

'Just about,' said Craig, concentrating on rubbing his calf and re-adjusting a shin pad, watching with pleasure as the ref flourished a yellow card over the defender. Then Craig glanced at the touchline. His mum hadn't run onto the pitch, but the look on her face said she might do so at any minute. 'Right, let's get this free kick taken,' he said hurriedly . . . but then he paused.

He realized it was Wayne who'd helped him up, asked if he was OK, and was still standing beside him, holding his arm. Craig looked him in the face, and suddenly he just didn't want to be angry with Wayne any more.

'I'll take it,' said Darren, coming up fast

behind them, carefully positioning the ball. They were ten metres outside the Warlington box and just in from the right touchline, the crowd suddenly buzzing with anticipation behind them. 'You two get up for this,' said Darren. 'Simple far-post ball, OK?'

Craig nodded to Wayne, who smiled and nodded back, and they ran into the Warlington area, yellow shirts jostling with black and red, the keeper yelling for a sight line. Craig knew there couldn't be much longer to go, he sensed the tension rising, he felt the power coursing through his muscles.

Darren curled the ball in beyond the keeper, Craig starting his run as Wayne leapt for it on the far post, beating a Warlington defender and getting in a header that sent the ball looping towards the penalty spot, Craig ghosting through the ruck of players to meet it perfectly with his forehead.

The ball flew past the keeper's despairing dive and billowed the net.

But Craig didn't stop running, he turned and raced out of the area back towards the right-hand touchline, arms outstretched, yelling wildly, crazily, ecstatically in triumph, Darren trying to grab him, Wayne following and screaming at his dad and jabbing at the City crest on his chest, the rest of the City lads strung out behind them, the gaffer standing arms folded, smiling.

It was 1–0 to the City, and that's the way it was going to stay.

EPILOGUE

Jimmy Shepherd opens his office door and goes inside, hangs his jacket on the hook behind it. He puts the kettle on, drops a teabag in his special mug, adds sugar, sits at his desk. He can hear cars revving outside, adults laughing and talking. He'll have to say goodbye to old Tony Rosemount before the Warlington lads leave on their coach, have another chat with the directors and the sponsors . . . But Jimmy likes a quiet moment after a match, a pause to collect his thoughts, go back over the game in his mind. These boys are shaping up nicely, he thinks, they've got loads of potential, more than any other group he's had before. A few problems, though, Wayne's dad among them, some sort of family trouble upsetting Craig, Darren's confidence a bit shaky at first. He'd be keeping an eye on Ben, too, who still needed to settle in, and Lee seems a bit under his dad's thumb . . . Anyway, it was a pretty good result,

Jimmy Shepherd thinks as the kettle boils, although not a perfect performance, not by any means. He pours the water over the teabag in his mug, decides to let his tea steep while he pops into the changing room. Time to bring his lads down to earth a little bit. They've still got plenty of work to do in training, he thinks. Oh yes, plenty of work . . .

If you enjoyed **UNDER PRESSURE**,
you might enjoy the next in the series:

BAD BOYS

TONY BRADMAN

HARD enough?

BEN's struggling to be accepted as one of the lads.
Can he toughen up his act?

LEE wants to make his own decisions — but just ends
up in deep trouble. And now Ben's targeted him...

It's a question of BOTTLE!

Don't miss this riveting novel of challenge and confrontation
— the second book to be set amongst the lads in a soccer
youth training group at City FC, home of the HAWKS.

0 552 547611

 Could *you* score for city?